JUSTICE FOR BELLE

DIDI OVIATT

To my amazing mom, Diane, thank you for your encouragement and support; without you, my writing would be a mere lost cause. To the very talented author TL Harty, a special thanks; this book wouldn't be what it is without you. Most importantly . . . Caleb, you're my rock, and our kids are my reason. Thanks for your patience and for putting up with my crap for all these years. I love you with all of me.

Didi

CHAPTER ONE

There's a gangly man who looks to be in his mid-forties sitting on the short, wrought-iron bench across from the identical one I'm wasting my afternoon on. It's midday Sunday, so the Amtrak station is busier than regular weekdays at this time. The weekend travelers are returning to their homes and their busy lifestyles here in Flint Michigan, no doubt. I'm not going to or coming from anywhere; I'm just here to people watch. I do this often when I need inspiration.

The man is tapping his long dress shoes nervously on the dirt-colored, industrial-grade carpet beneath our feet. He's definitely guilty of something or another, that or else he's in an anxious hurry. Either way, he clearly wants to flee the joint. He's probably a stabber.

I picture his wiry fingers gripped so tightly around the handle of a butcher knife that his protruding knuckles have whitened. The square shape of his jaw seems more prominent as his teeth are clenched. The whites of his sharp, ocean-blue eyes are glazed over, and one streak of crimson appears across his face.

It's a flawless image, definitely noteworthy. I think I'll name him Donovan. Donovan, the ex-convict, freshly escaped from the state penitentiary after being convicted of brutally murdering his family with a butcher knife and then storing their mutilated bodies in the family freezer. Yep, that'll do just fine.

Call me weird, obsessed, paranoid, twisted, or whatever, but I have this nasty little habit of trying to guess what kind of killers people would be . . . if they were actually killers, that is. Whenever I see someone in a crowd who stands out among the rest, I see it. It all depends on their size, the way they move, the look in their eyes. Everything plays a part, and the image is usually fairly detailed. Then, I jot down my observations for future use.

My dad's wife, Dorothy, blames it on my *'dark, overactive imagination, rooted from the death of my mother.'* Dorothy's a therapist, so naturally, she thinks she knows everything. My mom passed away seventeen years ago in a car accident. Two years after that, Dorothy came along, and she's been trying to fix us all ever since. I don't think she actually cares, though; it's clearly all for image's sake. There was nothing dark about my mom's passing; accidents are reality, and life flat-out sucks sometimes.

Dorothy is obviously overeducated and very seriously lacking in the common sense department. She cares more about money and image than anything, and Dad is too passive to shut her up. I really don't understand why anyone in their right mind would pay that woman hundreds of dollars an hour for her far-fetched opinions, or *'help'*, as she calls it. Point in fact, these people are NOT in their right mind. Therein lies the very definition of irony, I suppose. Don't get me wrong; I'm not completely anti-therapist. For every dozen, there is a dime. I've even been to a few shrinks of my own. Yet here I am, still constantly daydreaming about heinous death.

To make things even more conveniently cliché for dear Dorothy, my little brother was recently accepted into medical school. At age thirty, he's really making a comeback from our troublesome youth. I'm just waiting for Dorothy to make some crack about how his subconscious wants to save car accident victims to make up for the loss of our mother. That's really the only thing she has to play on, that she knows of.

No sooner do I finish writing down the details of Donovan burning his bloodied clothing in a backyard fire pit than a fresh, warm body accompanies me on my bench. He sits a little too close for comfort. Close enough that I can feel the warmth from his leg and smell him. The scent is delicious. *Doesn't anyone have boundaries anymore,* I think. I let my long, jet-black hair fall over my shoulder, concealing the side of my face. It doesn't help; I can still feel the fixation of his amused eyes, searing their way through my hair's shield. I can even sense him smiling. *Who does this weirdo think he is?*

"Can I help you, sir?" I ask, peeking past the edge of my loose waves so that he can see the irritated lift of my brows but nothing else.

He's handsome, very handsome. *Damn, of course he is.* Probably around my age too. The barely-formed crow's feet at the sides of his excited eyes scream early to mid-thirties. It's moments like this that I wish I didn't look less than half my age. Every time a man that appears to be as old as myself, or even slightly older, shows an interest, I automatically assume he's a creep for flirting with a teenage girl. I'll probably draw in pedophiles for the whole of my life. I could easily pass as a high school student any day of the week.

I'm sure that once I reach my sixties, I'll be grateful for my smooth, slightly olive skin that hasn't seemed to age since my childhood. The perks of being of mixed race to the point of not even knowing exactly where I come from. I have at least five generations of mixed heritage from all over the place. Some Hispanic, some Irish, some Italian . . . even a little Greek. Honestly, who knows what other sperm snuck its way into my family tree. We all look different. I'm not exactly dark, but I'm not white either, and my brother is as pale as one can possibly be, with fiery hair to match his freckles.

"Do I know you?" The perfect looking, boundaryless man asks.

His flawless teeth are on full display. The smile is assisted by the deepest dimples I've ever seen.

"Probably not."

"Are you sure? You look extremely familiar."

"Nah," I answer with a mumble and turn my attention back to the notebook on my lap. "I just have a common face," I say as I tap my pen on the page.

"No, you don't."

I can hear the smile behind his words. *Don't look up, Ahnia. Whatever you do, don't give in to the charm of this irritatingly attractive stranger.*

"Oh?" I ask. My gaze is glued to the notebook.

"Nope, not common at all. It's your eyes, I think; the green is like neon . . . and your lips too. You have distinct peaks. I've definitely seen you before. Trust me; I have a thing about faces. Especially pretty, detailed ones like yours."

Okay, now I'm intrigued. If nothing else, at least his approach is unique. I glance around my hair one more time. I can't really help myself. There's a tiny hint of stubble on the sides of his cheeks, and his hair is a wreck. It looks like he hasn't combed it . . . well, ever. I don't usually like the unkempt look, but for some inexplicable reason, it comes off as absolutely to die for on this man. He appears relaxed and carefree in a natural way.

Despite the messy hair, his clothes are clean, pressed even. And his smell, oh my God, his smell. The longer he sits so close, the more heavenly it seems. It's a fresh scent, like a light, rustic soap. Nothing too strong and overwhelming like most men who are trying to pick up girls in random public places like Amtrak stations. I hate that lingering aftershave scent, especially Old Spice. It makes me want to puke in my mouth.

I'm certain I've never met him. I'm entirely confident that I'd remember his face too. I look back down at my page, reading over my recent murder notes. I don't think I can watch him scratch at his chin in thought for one more second without caving into my urge to lean over and take a whiff of his shirt. Just to bury myself in its freshness and try to figure out what kind of laundry soap he uses. I might even go to a department store after this and sniff around the detergent aisle. I'd kill to smell like him right now.

"Hmmm . . ." he thinks aloud in a deep, humming voice as smooth as butter.

"You figure it out yet?" I ask dryly.

"Net yet. But don't you worry," he giggles, "I will. Whatcha' writing?"

I shoot him the same irritated glance as before. No words are given; I'm really just trying to build my shutout wall as high as possible. This guy is tenacious. He chuckles at me again, brushes my hair back over my shoulder, and then leans over my lap. He's now even further into my personal space.

Who the hell does he think he is? I don't fight it because his thumb just brushed against my collar bone in the gesture. The shocking chill it gave me has practically shut off my airwaves. There's absolutely no room for protest, or any words really.

No matter, as soon as he reads my morbid page, he'll go

running for the hills. What better way to tell a guy to piss off than to let him read a couple of random paragraphs describing the man sitting across from us as brutalizing his family with a butcher knife.

He reads the page and then leans back casually. A completely blank expression is plastered all over his face. Again, he scratches at the stubble, and looks forward at the nervous, skinny man tapping his foot on the floor.

Any second now. I'm waiting patiently with a smirk for him to stand up and make for a getaway. *Nothing.* He does nothing but nod and stare. Next comes the unthinkable. He reaches for my notebook and pen. Completely disregarding any reaction I might have, he sets to work. He begins scratching out words and filling in spaces around the page's mayhem with his own little intake on my notes.

"You had it all wrong," he says proudly, before handing me back the goods.

I look at the page to find he's changed the butcher knife to an axe and the scene of the crime to a holiday party. He's also changed the ages of Donovan's murdered kids, making them older. I think on the changes and stare at the real Donovan, whatever his name actually is. Somehow, it fits.

"I know, much better, right?" my new friend announces.

"Why, though?"

He turns to face me. Our featured inspiration is only a couple of feet away. He can clearly hear our conversation but remains oblivious to the fact that it's centered on him.

"Wide, strong shoulders. An axe is hard to swing, and he could totally pull it off."

I nod; it actually makes sense.

"Why the kids' ages?"

"Grey hair, age-spotted skin, he's older than you've given him credit for."

"Maybe he's younger than he looks."

"Maybe he's even old*er* . . ." He lifts a knowing, quizzical eyebrow.

"*Humph.* You're good at this."

"I know, and I figured it out."

He now has my full attention. I, too, turn to face him head on. We're within inches of each other, our legs pressed together. The peppermint from his chewing gum permeates the air around me with his every breath.

"Shoot," I say, giving the go ahead.

The space between our faces continues to shrink, and our eyes are locked. I smile back at him, but only with one side of my mouth. *This ought to be interesting.*

"Ahnia Airington."

"How did you know that? I swear to God I've never met you."

"Thirteen years ago. You were eighteen, and I was twenty. You accepted an award at a writing conference I attended. We didn't exactly meet, but you left an impression. I read your book, and I remember your face."

"That was a long time ago." I look back down at my useless notebook in shame.

My friend crosses his arms over his chest, and his proud grin lowers on one side. It's not even a smirk as much as an 'I told you so' look while waiting for some kind of explanation. One that I'll never give for that matter. *Ever.*

"Your book was good."

"I don't write anymore," I snap.

"Clearly," he says while pointing a finger at my notes. "So why'd you stop at one novel? It was a bestseller, remember? Award-worthy even, and at such a young age." Again, he scratches at his stubble. "What did they call you at that conference? A prodigy?"

"I have to go."

I clutch my notebook tightly against my chest and push through a crowd of soon-to-be Amtrak passengers by the exit sign.

"Wait," he calls from much closer behind me than I was hoping for.

My shoulder catches one of an elderly woman in passing. She scowls hard and lets out an angry *umph*. I don't apologize, but I can hear him mutter a 'sorry' on my behalf. Now I'm even more irritated. He recognized me from my prime, is also a writer, has read my work, is handsome, and now he has to be courteous too? I hate him already.

"Look, I didn't mean to cross any lines," he speaks over my shoulder as I shove open the door.

A breeze from the light wind catches my face, blowing a chunk of my hair behind my back. Of course he keeps at it as I make my way through a tight parking lot behind the station. My only choice is to stop before reaching my fairly old Volvo, or he'll likely help himself into the passenger seat the very second I press the unlock button. Finally, I spin on my heels to face him.

"My life is none of your business," I snap as I pull my notebook closer to my chest.

His cheeks frame that unfaltering grin.

"Are you always so mean to your fans?"

"Fan?"

I'm kind of caught off guard. I haven't heard the word "fan" in over a decade.

"Your book was good."

"Umm . . . thanks, I guess." I can feel my eyebrows involuntarily pull to the center of my face. "Look, I really do have to go. Thanks for being a fan, Mr. . . . .?"

I wait for an answer to the awkward way of my asking his name, but to my surprise, he only laughs at me . . . again.

"Mr.? Really? Do I look ninety?"

"Oh my God." My eyes do a full circle. "Never mind."

As I make a second attempt to flee, he grabs me softly at the elbow.

"Wait, sorry, sorry. I really am." He fails to completely stop the chuckles as they roll further from the base of his throat. "I didn't mean to laugh at you, really. I just don't think anyone has ever made me feel so old before. Maybe it's because you still look so young."

His eyes widen with an instant apology before he stumbles over his words.

"I mean, I'm sorry again. That's not what I meant. You *do* look young, but in a good way. I mean . . . damn it . . ."

He drops his forehead into an open palm. All I can do is stare. I can't really tell if he is making a fool of me or of himself. It's hard to say at this point, but for some reason, I can't seem to pull myself away. His clear stutter and embarrassment actually makes him look even more handsome. He then runs a hand through his messy hair and lets out an exasperated sigh.

"I'm Mac," he finally admits.

I take his offered hand in mine and give it a firm shake.

"It's nice to meet you, Mac. Now, if you'll excuse me, I'd like to forget that this entire conversation ever happened."

He clears the lump from his throat and nods with a disappointed understanding, yet doesn't argue. He even turns away before I do. I feel kind of lonely watching him disappear back into the station, which is weird. I don't usually feel much emotion, of any sort to be precise. I'm just not the emotional type.

He doesn't turn back around. He doesn't do a double take

over his shoulder. He just dumps his hands into his pockets, drops his chin to his chest, and walks off. This has positively been my weirdest encounter yet at the Amtrak station.

Next time, I'll do my observing at the mall, I think as I finally climb into my car and drive away.

CHAPTER TWO

R *ap Rap Rap*
"Ahnia!" Tim shouts as he pounds on my bedroom door. "Hurry it up in there! We're already running behind, and it's rush hour. Dorothy's going to have a fit if we're not sitting at the table by seven."

"Who gives a shit!?" I yell back at my persistent little brother, while I continue to rummage through my closet for something to wear. I'm completely unprepared and a little embarrassed with myself because of it. I hate all of my clothes, and I've recently gained weight.

Most everything I own makes me feel like an oompa loompa. I don't look like one at all. I'm actually the fairly average height of five foot and a couple of inches, quite well proportioned. My uncomfortable fifteen extra pounds settle mostly on my hips and bust, allowing me to keep my hourglass shape no matter what the number on a scale reads.

Dad's entire staff will be at dinner tonight, and I've already disappointed him enough. I really don't want to be any more uncomfortable than I'm already doomed to be, while everyone quizzes me about my intentions for the future. I haven't sold many books in the last few years. My best-selling thriller is slowly being forgotten, and I'm rapidly running out of the stockpile of cash funds I'd accumulated those first few years after its release.

"*You* might not care much, Ahnia. But I personally don't want to hear her complain about our disregard for her feelings all night. She made the reservations for this place two weeks ago, remember? We really don't need to give her any ammo to embarrass Dad with."

Damn, he's right.

"I'm hurrying, I promise. Two more minutes!"

"You said that ten minutes ago! And your couch sucks by the way. You probably should've just picked me up instead of the other way around. I would have left your ass by now."

"Go then!" I shout at the door.

He doesn't answer, but I know he isn't leaving me either. It's always the empty threats. My brother and I have been there for each other through thick and thin. He's my saving grace, and I'm that irritating weight on his back that he's too stubborn to let go of. My couch really does suck too; he has a good point. It's the same one I've had since my bar-hopping days.

For about three years straight, I lived like a fly. Bouncing around from bar to bar, picking up parties to take back home at all hours of the night. It's a miracle I survived the consistent drunken madness. I even made it past that phase of life unscathed. My furniture? Not so much.

I finally settle for a black satin piece. It's mid-calf so I can show off my favorite heels along with the pedicure I treated myself to yesterday, despite the dissipating end balance on my monthly bank statements.

Satin is a terrible fabric when you're self-conscious about your shape, but screw it. At least the sides are bunched so that my stomach pooch isn't so prominent. I pull the dress into place, buckle up my stilettos at the ankle, and do a quick once over on my face. A last round of powder is applied, one more layer of mascara is caked on, and a thick, velvety lipstick is carefully smeared into place.

If my body insists on being chubby, then at least my face can look deceptively flawless. Plus, the lipstick makes me look a tiny bit closer to my age, or I look like a kid trying her damnedest to appear of age in order to pave the way for imminent self-destruction.

The ride across town to Dad's company party goes as expected—slow, quiet. We're celebrating twenty-five years of active business at Airington's Treats. My father opened the place with my mother by way of encouragement on her cooking skills. Even after all these years, when I walk into my father's kitchen, I can picture her bare feet shuffling around and see the swirl of her spinning apron as she dances across the tile with her mixing bowl in hand. Despite her emotional troubles, my mom was always her happiest with good music blaring from the countertop while she baked.

Dad had received a medical settlement early on in their marriage, and after years of ups and downs with my mom's depression, he talked her into managing a new place to keep her spirits up. Apparently, a big project is highly encouraged by those shiny, worthwhile shrinks.

Mom loved to cook goodies and sweets, and Dad had just enough money left to dump on an utterly impractical investment. Five years in and she'd expanded the small eatery to three locations across the state. After she passed away, my father hired a new manager who, by some miracle, has been able to keep it afloat all this time. Her name is Madge, and she is a bitter old lady with a gruff voice.

Madge is always scowling and refusing to talk to anyone

about her personal life. I love Madge. Dad couldn't have picked a better lady to fill Mom's shoes in the business department.

Overall, I'm just glad Mom and Dad named the shockingly successful eatery Airington's rather than Aubrey's, like Dad wanted. He thought naming the place after her would really make it her own, but she refused to be so boastful as to name a business after herself. *Thank God.* How awkward would that have been, keeping a business that's named after your dead wife running for years after her passing? I'm sure Dorothy would've loved that.

Dorothy prides herself on Airington's success and takes full credit for its ratings from the public. She's never flipped on an oven or picked up a rolling pin in her life. Every recipe used to this date is still standing strong from Mom's personal "scratch only" collection. Dorothy is a phony, and Dad is a saint.

The event center Dorothy chose for Airington's twenty-fifth anniversary is rather extravagant, too much so in my opinion. But what does my opinion matter? According to Dorothy, I'm merely a washed-up artist on a downward spiral toward a lonely, poor life. I fear she could be right. Dad's offered me a job at one of Airington's locations on countless occasions, but I've declined the offer every time.

If I'm going to get paid minimum wage to bake cookies, then it sure as hell isn't going to be tied to my family in any way. I was once deemed a prodigy; if nothing else, that reserves me the right to refuse handouts. *I just need more time to get my head straight,* I try to convince myself.

"Are you ready for this?" Tim asks as he slides his Jeep into park.

I can see the underlining pity in his eyes. He knows as well as I do how the night will pan out. Everyone here will hug and congratulate Tim on his accomplishments and offer endless words of encouragement for his upcoming adventure into medical school. Then, they'll turn to me and ask if I've decided to write another book yet. To which I'll shrug my shoulders, and they'll giggle with fake smiles before they roll their eyes and drop their heads in shame behind my back.

"Ready as I'll ever be." My sarcasm is oozing.

"Don't let them get to you, Ahnia." He reaches over and squeezes my hand. "You'll write a book that's even better than your last one, and then everyone who's had any doubt in you can choke on everything bad they've ever said."

"We both know that will probably never happen."

"Why's that?" He lifts a brow.

"You know why," I mutter and refuse to let my eyes meet his.

"Whatever, Ahnia. You need to get that shit out of your head, and just do what you're good at . . . writing."

Tim is the only person who knows what really happened, what my best seller was based on. The fine line between reality, my nightmares, and my written novel explaining the grey area in between.

Her name was Belle, and I haven't had one single nightmare since the night I bashed her head in with a broken pipe from our garage. I can still feel the cold steel in my hand, and the thought of it makes my stomach flip. That night, Tim picked me up from her house blood-soaked, sleepwalking, and afraid. His tiny hands gripped the steering wheel of our father's car, and his little face could barely see over the dash. It was the same night Mom crashed while she was out looking for us. It was that very date that my nightmares stopped and my daydreams began.

I force myself back to reality, to the now.

"Shut up, oh mighty perfect one. Although, the thought of Dorothy pawing at her throat while she chokes on my success does kind of make me happy."

15

"Agreed," he chuckles. "Now let's get our asses in there and support Dad. Just stick with Madge, that ol' loon will chase off anyone looking for a conversation anyway."

"Yep, that's my plan."

The entryway is large with three men in suits taking coats and hanging them on hooks on the opposite side of a rounded corner. As if we're incapable of hanging our own, and one man isn't enough for the job. Their smiles are wide and their welcomes are as fake as the "gold" chain around my ankle.

"Are you here for the Airington's or for the MacConall's?" one of the coat thieves asks.

His eye contact is intense, his grin is full of sarcasm, and his pupils are enlarged. He's probably stoned, trying way too hard to act happy and normal while on the job. I'd sneak drugs too if I had to hang coats for a living. He'd be a creative killer; I see it right off. Probably slip some flesh-eating powder in the sleeve of a stranger's coat. Then he'd laugh about it later while he sucked every last cloud of smoke from the end of a skull-shaped bong.

"Airington." I smile back and place my hand through the offered hook of Tim's elbow.

"Right this way," the young man says; his smile stretches even closer to his ears.

We follow close behind, letting him lead the way. A large, stone archway opens the building up into a wide, double-sided conference space. Nearly a dozen catering carts split the two parties, as well as an empty stage, fully equipped with a built-in bar and a DJ station. I think it's a safe bet that Dorothy is to blame for the lack of a bartender on the Airington side, likely trying to avoid any kind of scene by an employee. Who cares if they'd have fun in the process, that woman would go to any length to remain in complete control at all times.

You'd think being a therapist she'd understand the concept of popping things that you've squeezed too tightly. It looks like

I'll be walking on the wild side tonight and making my way to the MacConall party.

"Children!" Dorothy's phony voice calls to us from across the room.

Dad smiles in our direction but remains respectably quiet. His fingers are laced together on top of the scarlet cloth of their table. The proud spark in his eyes is genuine. I cringe at the sound of her. You can tell that she's prepared herself to put on a show from the way she's talking a full octave above her normal tone. Tim gives her a wave before accepting a hug from Lucy, one of the bakers in Mom's original location, just a ten-minute drive from my own apartment.

Lucy is young, blonde, with gigantic blue saucer eyes, and an amazing baker. I give her a playful wink while they embrace, and she instinctively rolls her eyes. Lucy is practically my only friend, and I think she's had the hots for Tim since they first met. He won't listen to my urging him to ask Lucy out, though, despite the fact that she's a perfect catch. Whenever I bring it up, he only blushes and tells me to mind my own business.

I look away from Dorothy and her perfect posture with sprayed-stiff curls that barely touch her shoulders. I refuse to play into her show. Instead, I step behind the shield of my brother and Lucy and give a few friendly head nods to a couple of employees in the room while I scan the crowd for Madge.

I smile to myself when I spot her. She's sitting in the far corner by herself, scowling at Dorothy from across our side of the event center. Then she slips a young woman from the catering service a wad of cash and accepts a full bottle of vodka from behind the woman's back.

"I found Madge," I whisper to Tim after he loosens the embrace from another hug.

"Good luck," he whispers back. "I'll come and sit with you after I've made my rounds."

"Don't bother, just keep the wolves at bay. I'll be fine."

Tim only chuckles and reaches for my hand to give it a quick squeeze of reassurance. Our eyes meet and he squints, trying to read my thoughts no doubt.

"You sure?" he asks, low enough that no one else can hear. "You seem a little *off*."

"What do you mean *off*?" I demand under my breath.

"I don't know. You usually don't seem to give a shit. But today, you've been acting nervous."

I roll my eyes and let out a long, exaggerated sigh. Leave it to caring Tim to overthink every single aspect of the night, including my nerves. It's a shock that he's the younger one. Always taking care of his messed up big sister. Saving me from harsh critics, diverting Dorothy's judgment, and more . . . much more.

Hell, at the mere age of fourteen, he even cleaned Belle's blood from the car and the floor and woke up Dad to answer the front door. Then, he lied to the police about my being sick in the bathroom, while in reality, I was peeling bloody clothes from my shaking body.

Only the bathroom door separated his convincing lies from my disgusting truth on the other side. They hadn't even found Belle yet. They were there to tell us about Mom. Only Tim and I knew she was out looking for us. *She had to be.* We didn't even notice that her van was missing from the garage when we made it back home from Belle's house.

"I'll be fine, really," I assure Tim. "Maybe you should sit by Dad. One of us needs to do it, and I won't be able to share the vodka I just watched Madge bribe a caterer for if I'm that close to the warden."

Tim's laugh is infectious, but it only lasts for a moment before his face morphs into a deep scowl. Willing me not to overdo it with a warning stare. I giggle, wave a shooing hand in his direction, and do my best to ignore his comment as I walk away.

"Stay out of trouble, Sis." Tim only sort of teases, oblivious to the dark memories my mind has wandered to.

Madge slides out the chair for me that's next to hers, but her leathered face doesn't falter. Gladly, I take the seat and join her for a moment of silence. The sarcasm that I love so dearly about Madge is boiling under the surface. I can tell already that her kettle is about to blow.

The same woman who'd slipped her the bottle of booze makes her way back to our table, balancing a tray complete with pitchers of iced water and soda. The glasses in front of Madge and myself are filled quickly with something clear and bubbly, but only halfway and without asking first what we'd like. I don't oppose; I assume Madge has already given the girl strict instructions. I completely trust her judgment. It's probably Sprite or tonic water. Either will do just fine.

Casually, and without being asked, I grab both glasses and hold them under the table for Madge to top off with her hidden contraband. Our actions go unnoticed, and we're ready to move forward into the night of pending doom. I smile and take a sip.

"I'm glad you've prepared," I finally break the silence.

"You know me," her gruff voice cracks before she, too, takes a swallow. "This is some good soda."

"Did you call beforehand, or threaten the poor girl with her life once you got here?"

"Does a bear shit in the woods?"

Her analogy makes little sense in this circumstance, but I appreciate the comeback either way. I smile and we clink our glasses together. The pre-twitch of a grin plays at the corner of Madge's wrinkly lips. I imagine her to kill a different way every time, yet she'd always top off the event with that reserved grin of pride and satisfaction.

"Just look at him," I say, motioning my glass toward Tim. "He's so at ease at these things. Sometimes I wonder if we're even family."

Together, Madge and I watch as at least one person from each table rises to their feet to congratulate him and either shake hands or hug him on his way past. He knows them all by name and holds short but genuine conversations with each and every person he encounters. Madge lets out a huff of scratchy air and pulls her shoulders up to her ears.

"You're smarter."

"I'm washed up—he's going to medical school. How many of these bottles did you sneak before I got here?"

"Nah, he just applies himself. You're still smarter."

Madge ignores my question, as usual. She really only talks about what she wants, when she wants. If the topic, or even the tease doesn't fit into her momentary thought process, then it's brushed aside. It never fails, and it doesn't matter who she's talking to. All conversations go the way Madge wants them to, period. I wish I had her tenacity.

Tim takes a seat next to Dad. Both of their faces immediately point my way. Large smiles fill their cheeks. I return the gesture and wave at them. Dorothy, who's tentatively on the other side of Dad, lowers her eyes as she watches the display of family bonding, a bond that's completely excluded her. The two of them, both giving me their utter attention from across the room, while she's a mere two feet away, will never do.

She pulls herself to a stand, straightens her expensive navy blue pantsuit with the palm of her hands, and then begins to tap a spoon against her Shirley Temple glass. She's holding it in the air like they do in the movies, but only the movies. Sometimes I wonder what kind of fantasy world she lives in.

The room silences, and all eyes are now on Dorothy. She unnecessarily clears her throat before speaking.

"Thank you all for coming tonight. What a crowd!"

Everyone claps, some more enthusiastically than others. Dorothy nods and grins, absorbing the applause like a moist sponge on spilled water. She has a full and satisfied look as if the clapping is actually intended for her personally. It wouldn't surprise me if she started sprouting overflow water from her ears.

"First item of business, Damian and I would like to thank you all for another wonderful year of success at Airington's Treats."

Dorothy raises her hands, and starts the second round of applause herself. I watch my dad closely. Pride seeps through his face as he scans the room. It shows thick in the watering of his eyes and the purse of his lips. His forehead is lifted into a few wrinkles at his thinning hairline. He looks every bit his age.

I watch as he slowly wrings his hands atop the table. He doesn't join the applause but humbly absorbs it. Every year at the anniversary party, I sit as far from Dorothy as I can and allow myself to feel homesick for Mom.

Two people died *that* night, and both were my fault. I wish I didn't sleepwalk, and I wish I could remember exactly what happened under the blanket of that night's darkness. Most of all, I wish Mom were here now to see her business flourish. Airington's Treats was her baby, second only to myself and Tim. She loved to bake and she loved the eatery. I can only imagine it to be her giving the speech of gratitude in a room full of content employees, rather than Dorothy.

I tune out the rest of Dorothy's babbling as two familiar faces catch my attention. My chest drops to the pit of my stomach in one swift motion and stays there. Over on the MacConall side of the event center, a whole different chain of events is playing out. There is also a round of applause, but it's in the far corner of their space. Luckily, it doesn't take away from Dad's party in any way. I'm still distracted by it because of *them*. I can't quite make out what they are saying, but I don't need to.

It takes a couple of tries to swallow the lump in my throat as familiar face number one drops to one knee. He holds a velvet box in the air, containing a shiny rock on a silver ring. It's pointed in the direction of familiar face number two. Only number two isn't familiar because I know her. She's familiar because she looks exactly like me.

We have identical neon-green eyes that stand out from a distance. Her lips peek in the exact fashion as my own. Her hair is long, thick, and black, spilling over one shoulder untamed. The likeness of this woman and myself makes me a little dizzy.

I watch *them* closely, completely oblivious to Dorothy and the party I should be mentally attending, but I can't. My mind is racing, until it stops and the only comprehensive thought in my brain is, *no fucking way!* My doppelganger cries, nods her head, and lets the man slip the shiny ring on her finger. Then he pulls himself up, engulfing her into a hug and a spin.

As soon as her feet touch back to the floor, he lifts his glass into the air, looks right over to our side of the conference center, and allows his handsome gaze to land on mine. Our eyes lock instantly. Time stands still long enough that if it were a pond, it'd likely grow stagnant. I freeze in place, molding into my chair; the air is stuck in my lungs. He smiles as big as Superman . . . mission accomplished. Then he winks at me before handing his attention, and life, back to his new fiancé.

An old man at their table stands to give them each a hug. His deep, aged voice carries into the quiet of their crowd, just loud enough for me to hear the words from our side of the event center.

"Welcome to our family, Mac."

CHAPTER THREE

Despite the delicious scent of freshly baked cinnamon rolls that Lucy just pulled from the oven, nausea sweeps through me. A salty line of cold sweat beads are forming on the upper outline of my top lip. It's been a week since Dad's party, and the queasy feeling returns to my body every time I recall the haunting wink I got from Mac after he proposed to that woman who looks exactly like me. His words from that day at the Amtrak station ring over and over in my ears. *"Trust me; I have a thing about faces. Especially pretty, detailed ones like yours."*

In the far corner, opposite the restrooms, I sit and stew. The screen from my laptop stares at me, taunting me. Multiple tabs are pulled up. The one and only tab I should be focused on leads to nothing but a blank document, absent the writing that I aspire to do. I couldn't concentrate in my apartment this morning, so here I am.

I dread the inevitable day when I find myself out of cash, as that day is rapidly approaching. I really do want nothing more than to produce something, anything, but I'm grasping at straws. My notebook of fictional killers based on real people sits off to the side of my PC's keyboard, splayed out and flipped through a hundred times over. Yet, not a word of it has been transformed into anything useful or novel-worthy.

After pissing around on the internet for a couple of hours this morning, mostly on one particular site that has nothing to do with my own writing, I thought food might help. My kitchen is usually empty, aside from a few packages of twenty-five-cent processed noodles in a styrofoam cup and a couple of fat-free yogurts that will likely expire before they're eaten. I found myself tucking my PC into a backpack and making my way to Airington's, as usual.

One of the perks of having the family business is that it provides an endless supply of free food. For the most part, I've spent years trying to pace myself with this delicious convenience. Lately, I couldn't care less about the sugar and carbs. I'm broke, so screw it. Who cares if I wind up with a few more pounds in the mid-section? There's no one to impress. As long as my stomach doesn't grow any bigger than my rear end, I'll cope. Free food is free food, so you won't hear a complaint from me.

I let my teeth sink into the delicious edge of a glazed donut and continue to stare at all the open tabs across the top of my screen. One in particular is calling to me. It's the same webpage I've spent most of the week memorizing. It's one that Madge's granddaughter, the vodka smuggling caterer, pointed me to. She watched my face practically fold from a few tables away, while topping off a glass of sparkling cider. Apparently, the girl's an observant little sneak, bless her heart.

I pull the business card she'd slipped me from out of my back pocket and read over the note she'd plastered on the blank side:

. . .

24

A friend of my grandma is a friend of mine. We both know she doesn't have many. I noticed the look on your face when your twinner got engaged. Hope this helps.

I read the words over a few times, *your twinner, your twinner, your twinner.* I knew I wasn't crazy for seeing the resemblance. I don't understand how it's possible. I flip the card over to its top side and rub my thumb across Mac's face. MacConall's Marketing Management, the card reads. His real name is actually Mackenzie MacConall. What the shit kind of name is that, anyway? No wonder he goes by Mac. The business name on the card is followed by a main business website, a couple phone numbers, and a slew of social media links. I shake my head and let out an exasperated breath of air.

I shove the card back into my pocket and force my attention to its rightful place on the computer. The temptation of that one particular open tab shouts out at me. One of my hands soon begins to drum its fingers on the table, while the other rubs its sweaty palm on my jeans. I can't take it. Just one more look, and then I'll exit out of this site for good.

The tab is clicked on, and their faces are instantly staring back at me, with a quote from the alluring Mac himself:

> *"MacConnall Marketing Management will soon be expanding the family business. Two families joining together. Because that is what we are as a business . . . family." – Mac*

Who in the actual shit uses a marriage engagement as an

advertisement tool? And for a marketing business? Takes a real lack of couth to be so bold. It seems a little tacky for my taste. I pulled this site up that very night the second I got home. The couple's photo was already there, as well as Mac's cheesy line. The photo was clearly taken by a professional in a time when the mountains in the background were still tipped with snow.

That had to have been at least two months ago. Yet, the engagement ring on her finger catches the light of the sun just enough to prove that their entire episode that night was for show. Surprised, happy tears and a fairytale twirl, my ass. *Well played Mac, well played, but I'm onto your lie.*

Granted, I've only spoken to him once, but I wouldn't have taken him for a phony. Invasive, yes . . . irritating, absolutely. But a phony? I never saw it coming. If it wasn't for his new fiancé looking like my double, I'd have forgotten about the entire coincidence of his engagement coinciding with Dad's party. Forgotten entirely about Mac altogether. But because of *her,* I can't.

Now here I am, obsessing over their photo. His words still bouncing in and out of my head like a kid's bouncy ball. His wink still haunting my thoughts. Even his smell keeps randomly assaulting my nostrils. Perhaps I imagined it, but I swear the woman pumping gas next to me last night had to use the same detergent he does.

Before I can close out the tab, Lucy plops herself onto the heavily-padded, round bench next to me. I didn't see her walking over. I was too consumed by the engagement photo of Mac and his lady. I fumble my fingers around, trying to navigate the mouse to that tiny 'x' in the corner. It does no good. She's already seen what I'm looking at. Any further action would only draw more attention to myself. I'm thoroughly busted.

"Hey, you know that guy?" she asks, a pointer jabbing at his face.

"Nope." It's only kind of a lie.

"Ooooohhhhhh."

A lone wrinkle forms at the top of Lucy's pulled-up nose. She moves her face a little closer to inspect the lucky lady in Mac's arms. He's draped over the woman's back like a comfort blanket.

"Wow, do you know her? I didn't realize Mac had a girl. She looks exactly like you . . . weird."

Words catch in the back of my throat. I don't even know where to start. Should I answer her question, lash out about the girl, or inquire exactly how she knows Mac? It can't be coincidence, the way his name rolled so casually off of her tongue.

Lucy leans back in her chair and takes a long sip of her cappuccino. Her pretty, ocean-blue eyes fixated on my face, waiting for a response. I follow suit, taking a sip of my own hot beverage, letting my silence speak for itself.

"You looking for a marketing firm?" she asks; a smile plays at the corner of her lips.

I can feel my ears darken in a blush. I shrug and continue to stare at *them*, refusing to let Lucy see my face full on.

"I'm on break," she continues, "and I have nothing to do for the next fifteen minutes until that buzzer sounds to tell me my apple pie is finished."

"What's your point?"

"You can ignore me all day, but embarrassment is written all over that cutsie, little face of yours." She waves a wild finger in the air as if to prove a point. "I think I'll just sit here until you crack."

I sigh and drop my chin to my chest. A sure sign of surrender. Lucy is the closest thing to a friend that I have, besides Tim and Madge. She's sweet, fun, and easy to talk to. But she's relentless. Positively the most nosy girl I've ever met. It isn't always a bad thing because she forces me out of my introverted shell. But it's days like today that I crave her silence just as much as I do her companionship.

I can't bear to open my mouth and say the words, yet I want to scream at the top of my lungs. I want to shout about how I don't know him, but I can't stop thinking about him. I can't get his face out of my head.

I want to break down and tell her that the last time I was obsessed over two single humans, I was sixteen and I killed the girl in my sleep. I want to tell her about the way Tim came to my rescue that night. He drove our Dad's car after having snuck it out of the garage. I want to cry and beg and demand answers about the woman with my face. *Who is this bitch that's engulfed in Mac's arms?*

"You know Mac?" I finally croak, still refusing to look over.

"Not really, but yeah, I guess. He's been coming in every morning this week. Ever since he heard of the place."

I nod to myself, connecting the dots while she continues.

"I guess sharing an event center wasn't all bad. If nothing else, it brought us in new customers."

"Hmmm."

"Your turn."

"What do you mean?" I ask, knowing exactly what she's referring to.

Lucy leans forward into my space and grins before nudging my leg. She looks like an adorable puppy ready to chase a ball.

"What's with the blush?" she beams. Then her smile fades to accompany the grim lowering of her brows. "And who is that girl?"

"I honestly don't know."

"You don't know about the blush? Or the girl?"

"Either?"

I tilt my head to the side, asking myself Lucy's same questions. What *is* with the blush, and who *is* this girl? The sound of Lucy's playful chuckle is a needle prick to my eardrums. It's all I can do not to wince.

"You know, I've seen him at the mall too," she hints, "twice this week."

"So?"

"Soooooo, I just thought you might like to know that piece of information."

"Why would I care about some stranger's shopping habits?"

"Why are you stalking his business page?"

This batting back and forth is pointless. A part of me knows that Lucy won't stop until she has some sort of answer to scratch that itchy curiosity of hers. So, I decide to give her something.

"I met him at the Amtrak station." I finally crack. "Then all of the sudden, out of nowhere, he shows up at that conference center, and I watch him propose to some girl that looks exactly like me."

Lucy's eyes widen and her lips part as she listens. She's clearly intrigued. I'm not surprised at all to the fact that she's instantly formulated a plan . . . for me.

"You know what this means, right?"

"No. But, I have a feeling you're going to tell me."

"We have to follow him! Like spies."

This makes no sense, but I'll play along. Whatever she is plotting might just get me some sort of answers too. Her motive could be rooted from her nosy tendencies, or even boredom, who knows. Either way, I could use the help in getting my own itch scratched. Plus, it'll give Lucy a project outside of trying to talk me into dinner dates that I can't afford with random guys I've never met and have no interest in holding conversations with.

So the plan sets in motion. Lucy and I agree that we have to find out why Mac has recently moved his business from Florida to Michigan, as the website states. We also have to find out why his fiancé looks so much like me, and why he's so interested in this particular bakery. More importantly, why exactly can't I stop obsessing over him? Lucy is animated, wanting me to follow him around like some sneaky fool. I insist on a more practical approach. Something a little less obvious, and a little more productive.

"Why don't I just come here a little earlier than usual? You said he's been stopping in every morning, right?"

"Yeah." She rolls her eyes.

"So can't I just casually run into him and have a normal conversation? Like a normal human?"

Lucy sighs. She's let down but compliant nonetheless.

"You're boring, but I guess you're right."

"How is being normal boring?" I ask with a chuckle.

"For one, you're not normal. For two, don't you think he's going to lie anyway? I mean, I don't know about you, but I really think spying will be much more productive."

"Why would he lie?" I ask.

Lucy always thinks people are hiding things, and she's completely fascinated by it. She's the only person who knows about my daydreams and murder notes who doesn't judge me for it. Aside from Tim, that is. Her energy is buzzing, and she leans forward for a more intense effect on our conversation. Her eyes are wide, both hands are cupping her coffee as if she prays to it, and her knee bounces ever so slightly from her nervous foot on the floor.

"There has to be something you're not telling me. And just look at his girl. She's your double, Ahnia! This whole thing is sketchy. I can feel it."

"Just like you could feel the Trump and Clinton conspiracy, right?"

"Hey, that shit is real."

Lucy's eyes grow even wider, and she playfully looks over her shoulder. I sense my own eyes smiling from my cheeks, and I purse my lips together to stifle my reaction to her ridiculousness.

"Okay, okay. He did compliment my features and mention having a thing for faces. Whatever that's supposed to mean."

"I knew it!" She huffs. "I told you, he's hiding something. Who says that kind of shit to a woman who looks exactly like his wife-to-be?"

"He also said he went to a writing conference years ago, yet he's in marketing."

We're both buried in our own thoughts, overthinking things. Lucy tends to have that effect. Talk about the ultimate over-analyzer. The sound of Lucy's oven timer snaps us back. She jumps to her feet, takes one more sip of her coffee, and then shoots me a seriously penetrating stare.

"Tomorrow morning, seven o'clock."

"Seven, really?"

I groan at the thought of it. I never roll my lazy ass out of bed before ten, ever. I don't have a job or kids to force such an action. Chirpy, morning people drive me batty, and it seems Lucy is the leader of the morning person pack.

"Seven!" Lucy repeats the time while pointing a finger in my personal space, again.

"Fine," I mumble.

I watch Lucy disappear into the kitchen, leaving me to my thoughts. If she were ever to kill someone, she'd probably tie them up and torture them, demanding some sort of answers to a conspiracy before finishing them off.

As usual, she's managed to change everything with a single

conversation. I force myself to close out the tab on my computer. I suppose she's right. It's time to stop obsessing, and take action. Who knows what tomorrow will bring.

I scarf down the rest of my donut and gulp the last of my beverage in one swallow before aimlessly flipping through the pages in my notebook for the thousandth time. Much like before Lucy's intrusion, I have no inspiration. No worthwhile storyline comes to my immediate attention.

It doesn't do me any more good today than it did yesterday, or even the day before to flip through these worthless notes. I have to get out of this place and away from Lucy before she's officially off the clock. Lord knows what will happen if she makes a second attempt at talking me into a trip to the mall.

My phone comes to life with a call. It moves across the table like an inchworm with its vibration. I continue shoving my notebook into my pack. I don't need to look at the screen to know who's calling. Douglas, my financial advisor, is the only person I've set with a ring tone of such doom and gloom as Beethoven's finest.

He was a friend of my mom's as a kid, which is the only reason he's stuck with me for this long. Guilt can be milked out much further than practically any other emotion. Or so I've learned over the years of dragging Douglas along.

"Shit," I mumble loud enough for only myself to hear.

Douglas has been trying to get ahold of me for weeks, and I've blown him off. He even went as far as to stop by my apartment. I'm sure he heard me walking around inside, but when I saw it was him out the peephole of the door, I held my breath and froze in place. I waited there like a statue, imagining my feet as being a concrete block on the floor. I even tried not to breathe until he gave up and left. It worked, but I can only avoid the persistent old number-cruncher for so long. His calls have progressed from once every couple of weeks to just about every day now.

I make a bet to myself on whether he'll leave a voicemail or just hang up and text me instead. My lime green pack is heaved over my back, supported perfectly by both shoulders. Then I shove the phone into my back pocket and make my way to the counter to steal one more donut from what's supposed to be a display on my way out.

Lucy is borderline obsessive-compulsive, so I'm sure she'll replace the treat and have everything back to its rightful order within minutes. It's too bad I'm not in a more playful mood. It's tempting to make a quick run into the bathroom to flip the toilet paper roll over. She hates it when the roll is upside down. I decide against it, at least for today, and leave.

The ping of a text grabs my attention before I fully step outside into the sweltering summer heat. It's from Douglas, of course, and it reads:

D—Ahnia, you can't avoid me forever. Please meet up with me. The sooner the better, I really don't want to do this by voice message or text.

Do this? What the hell does he mean? He's probably going to quit. That's really the logical thing. I wouldn't blame him. The money is nearly gone; he has no reason to stick around. I let out a sigh before texting him back. I'm going to have to adult up and deal with this sometime, right? Why not two shitty encounters all in one day? The big whammy. Knock out the two most mortifying events of my foreseeable future all at once to get them over with. And on a morning that I have to set an alarm. That seems fitting. I text him back.

A—I'll be at the eatery at 7:30 a.m. tomorrow.

I don't wait for another text back, and if he sends one, I won't acknowledge it anyway. If he does want to talk in person, then he'll make it work. It's the best I can do given my rocky emotional state. Plus, he's always early. Always. So it'll give me an excuse to get away from Mac, if need be. The rest of the day ahead will surely be full of stress and obsession.

I might as well get home so that I can wallow properly with the twenty pack of beer in my fridge that I'd snuck past Tim. Maybe later I'll even call in a pizza. Splurge on cheap alcohol and carbs to help bury my nerves and self-pity. I tuck my phone back into my pocket and force my feet to move forward.

CHAPTER FOUR

I'd hit snooze a few times, and now I'm running late. I should
have known this would happen. Of course I'd struggle to
wake up merely to the sound of the high-pitched beeping tone
of an alarm clock I've never used. Tim used to tease me as kids
that I needed a freight train running through my room to wake
me. Being such a hard sleeper is just one of my many curses.

I'm impossible to wake, which is why I made it eight whole
blocks on a sleepwalk *that* night, as well as the few others
before it. It was a miracle that Tim heard me pass his room. I'm
convinced that if my nightmares and sleepwalking wouldn't
have stopped after that night, then he surely would've followed
me through the years. I could picture him renting an apartment
right next to mine to this day.

My brother is my savior in every way. He's the only reason
I wasn't caught red-handed that night, and the only person
who's managed to keep me sane since, instilling me with words
of wisdom on a regular basis.

Even when my drinking problem spiraled to an uncon-
trolled low, he showed up one day to dump every last drop of

liquor down the metal drain of my tiny kitchen sink. Then, he refused to leave my side for weeks. We played more board games than I'd ever admit out loud. He won't put up with another downward drinking spiral, no way.

Tim knew which way I'd go *that* night. It was the same direction I went every time I walked. Directly to Belle's house. He'd picked me up three other times before. Each time, I'd been standing outside Belle's window when he found me. And each time, he was able to get me back home, undetected. Dad never knew his car went missing. Breakfast in the morning was always as usual. God, how I wish it would have been the same *that* night too.

A thick, square brush is forced through my wild hair before I tie it all in a giant knot on the top of my head. I scrub my teeth much harder than usual, in a hurry to get out. With a slam, the door shuts behind me. I don't even turn to lock the deadbolt with my key. The itty, bitty twister lock on the inside handle will just have to do. Besides, what kind of criminal would possibly be out at 6:50 in the morning? Only a killer worthy of my notes, no doubt, and I wouldn't even be here to observe it. Not only that, but what would they take? My couch? They can have it.

I don't even know why I deadbolt the door on a regular day anyway. It may be a small, outdated place with old, crimson carpet, and mustard-yellow countertops, but at least it's in a decent neighborhood. Not a high-class suburb like I grew up in, by no means, but not exactly dicey either.

Aside from Henry, the tax processor and his extremely friendly partner across the hall, everyone else in the building is old enough for retirement. They likely spend their days kicked back in a recliner glued to the TLC channel. I've tried several times to picture them, Henry and Jason the deadly duo, each pulling the trigger to a pistol behind the back of a kneeling victim, or something equally as tedious. The image never has stuck, so I'm quite sure there's nothing to worry about.

Just my luck, I hit every single red light on the way to Airington's. By the time I park my car and hop out, it's ten minutes after seven. It could've been worse. Ten minutes late really isn't so bad. Plus, it's not like this is a date. It's more like my cornering a guy that I've had one awkward conversation with, based on an assumption that he'll even be here at all.

I twirl between my fingers a strand of hair that's somehow managed to loosen itself from the knot on my head before tucking it back into its rightful place. Wanting to sprint across the street as not to give Lucy means for a scolding about my tardiness, I have to force my feet to slow.

As I swing open the door to Airington's, I'm greeted instantly by a face only inches from my own. I jump and gasp, startled not only by his closeness but by the scent of him. The same delicious smell that assaulted my very being at the Amtrak station makes a second strike. Like a brick wall, it stops me dead in my tracks.

There is no fumbling around with words or even catching of breath on his part. He stands his ground, an inch inside the door, his toes practically touching the metal frame it fits in. He has a styrofoam cup of coffee in one hand and a small white paper bag with his goodie of choice in the other. Mac grins, eyes lighting up, as if he's face to face with a fully lit Christmas tree rather than a wild-haired, pajama-wearing failure of an adult.

"Hey," he breaks the silence, voice as deep and smooth as ever.

"Hi," I crack in response.

"I was starting to wonder if you ever come here."

"It's seven in the morning. No one comes here this early."

This is already going opposite of my expectations. He appears cool and collected in his stance with an underlining excitement in the lift of his cheekbones. It feels almost like he was expecting me.

"I think the couple of regulars inside, as well as myself, beg to differ."

We're still blocking the entrance. The door is wide open. It's propped with my stiffened arm and held in place by my shaking hand. The banter is weird but engrossing. I don't think I've blinked, and I'm positive he hasn't. So many questions are forming in my mind, yet the first one I incoherently blurt out is:

"How do *you* know they're regulars?"

"How did you know I'd be here?" he fires back, grin widening.

"Answer my question."

"Answer mine first."

"I didn't know you'd be here."

"You're lying."

"I never lie."

I cringe at my own words, feeling the color change in my face. I even suck in the meaty middle of my bottom lip and give it a sharp bite. Punishment for being so crass. Practically everything about my life is a lie. Yet, here I am, staring into one of the most handsome faces I've ever seen, lying about lying. His squared shoulders, deepening dimples, and messy hair are causing my stomach to knot. I can only hope the weakening of my knees isn't showing on the outside.

"You *are* lying, because why else would *you* be here at seven in the morning? You wanted to see me, huh?"

I have no idea how this intense, doorway, stare-down conversation has transformed into this. I choke a little on the spit that's stuck in the back of my throat. Finally, I roll my eyes and slam my free hand on my hip.

"Are you going to move so I can get in or not?"

"You hungry?" He chuckles.

"Yes. Hence the reason I'm here." I continue to stare.

Mac finally steps aside and sweeps a welcoming arm through the air. He's clearly careful not to spill his coffee with the motion.

"I'll join you," he says.

There's an upbeat and excited twang in his words —irritating.

"Oh great, because the way you were headed out, I would have assumed you were leaving."

His scent follows close behind me. As soon as I'm able to get around him, I can see both Madge and Lucy behind the counter. Madge is ready to take orders and run the register. Lucy is unloading a fresh sheet of apple fritters. Raquelle, Lucy's usual morning helper must have called in again. Poor Madge is too old and has far more important things to do than to have to fill in for Raquelle.

At least Madge won't care to question why I'm here so early, or even who I talk to. She's private, and shows everyone else the same respect. Lucy, on the other hand, has been watching us like a hawk, within a very clear hearing range. Her jaw is practically sweeping the floor.

Mac points across the room. "I'll be waiting, right over there."

Of course he assumes I'm going to sit with him; what an egotistical douchebag. But then again, I *am* here for him, and I *will* sit with him. *So, what does that make me, I wonder? A sucker? A cliché?* I shoot Lucy a confused glare, willing her to read my mind. With big facial movements, she mouths the words 'I know' and then shrugs while pulling her bottom lip down at one corner to show a few teeth. Dramatic and silently, she shares my confusion. I shake my head slightly.

"What'll it be, love?" Madge asks with her regular straight face and in her notoriously scratchy voice.

"Surprise me."

I smile at her. She just nods and gets to slicing up a treat before dishing it onto a square plate.

I have no idea what to expect out of this peculiar morning, but there is one thing I do know for sure—I'm utterly attracted to Mac. I can't do anything about it because of *that woman* who's strangely my double. Everything about her screams Belle, and everything about Mac reflects my high school boyfriend. Aside from his hair and his smell, he could easily be an aged version of Charles. My first kiss, first love, and the first guy I ever killed for. Even if it was in my sleep, and even if he never actually knew it was me who swung the pipe that crushed Belle's skull.

I killed because of Charles and my subconscious obsession over how he looked at her because he wanted her more than he wanted me. Belle and I were so much alike. Same hair, same eyes . . . *just like the woman wearing Mac's ring.* Ultimately, Charles wound up dumping me on my ass a month later for a girl in the grade beneath us who had bigger tits and a wider smile. A girl who looked nothing like me, *or Belle, or Mac's girl.*

Mac and his fiancé are a terrible formula for me. One that's all too familiar. I'm afraid for Mac, afraid for myself, and mostly afraid for *her.* If I had any sense at all, I'd run, now. I'd make a screaming dash for the door and never look back. Instead, I reach for the free cheesecake Madge hands me over the counter, and I turn on my heels to join him.

He's waiting, sipping coffee and nibbling the edges of a bear claw while he watches me. I make a conscious effort to play it cool and casual, despite the extra strong thump of my heart and the tingling of my toes. I take a seat directly across from him in a tall, two-person booth that's pushed up against the one and only floor-to-ceiling window. It's the only table that's in perfect view from the outside passersby. I wish my hair was down so that I could hide behind it. Eating at this table is like being on display. It's a table I always avoid. I can only imagine that Mac doesn't care because if anyone were to see him, they'd assume that I was her and just keep on passing by.

I remain quiet, refusing to look him in the eyes. I know if I do that, then I won't be able to look back away. Instead, I glide my fork into the creamy white treat smothered with thick raspberry topping and shove it into my mouth.

Mac leans forward, pressing the weight of his shoulders on the table through his elbows. His strong fingers interlace each other and his palms are pressed together. Like the flash of a camera, I see it. This is different than my usual imaginings of murder. It seems a little more real, more unnerving.

Mac's muscular fingers are flexed, restricting the airway of another man. The neck within his grasp leads to a head that's as limp as a ragdoll. It's blurry, I can't make out the victim's details, but his entire head is flopping back and forth violently. Mac's face holds the same grin he's wearing now, except his teeth are clenched tighter, causing the vein in his neck to bulge. His voice interrupts the image, and I snap back to reality.

"Let's get to it, shall we?" he says.

I laugh despite myself, covering my mouth with a hand to ensure my food doesn't go flying into his face.

"Get to what?" I ask, forcing my vicious mental intrusion to the back of all the other swarming thoughts in my head.

I'm finally starting to become at ease with my body's nerves, but my mind is racing. I wonder how the hell I'm going to get the upper hand on wherever this strange conversation is going. As well as get a handle on how real that vision of him murdering a man actually seemed.

You're smarter than this guy, Ahnia, I tell myself. *He's a stranger, and engaged, and you have no right to have feelings for him or take serious your daydreams, and especially no right to play into whatever strange fixation he has for you.*

"Get to why you're here this early in the morning. No lies this time. You knew I'd be here, didn't you?"

"Are you saying you've been coming here on purpose . . . as bait for me?" I ask and shovel another bite in my mouth.

He shrugs and lifts a questionable brow. I swallow the mouthful of cheesecake that's rolling around on my tongue with a gulp. After which I force myself to match his wit. If he wants to play this game, then so be it.

"For your information, Mac, I'm meeting my financial advisor." I take a third bite, eating like the poor, hungry girl I really am and continue with a full mouth, "He'll be here any minute."

Now it's Mac's turn to laugh. He even leans back and runs a hand through his wild hair before folding his arms over his chest. I can only hope for Douglas to be his usual, punctual self. I could really go for a rescuing right about now.

"I'm sure he is." Mac rolls his eyes before allowing his face to smooth over. "Look Ahnia, I do, in fact, have a busy day, so I'm not going to waste a bunch of time. I *have* been coming here hoping you'll eventually show up early one day, and I'm glad you took the bait because I have a proposition for you."

I can feel my mouth open a crack, shocked by his honesty. I consciously shut it, and put my best sarcastic face on display.

"Oh really?" I say with a voice as flat as paper.

"Yes."

"What makes you think I want to do anything for you?"

I lean back in my chair and fold my arms across my chest too, mirroring his posture in every way.

"Because I know why you write about death in your little notebook."

I can feel my face tighten. My eyes lower to a slit and my lips pinch in anger.

"What the fuck are you talking about?" I ask under my breath.

"I know a lot about you, Ahnia. More than you think, and more than can be found on a simple Google search. The whole reason I'm in Michigan is, in fact, for you."

It feels like my heart is going to break free of my ribcage and bounce out of the huge window we're sitting by. My toes no longer tingle; they've become numb, as have the bottom half of my legs. I'm entirely stiff. What could he possibly know about me? Belle's face is front and center in my mind. *No.* No way could he know anything about her.

Play it cool, Ahnia; you have nothing to hide. Nothing but Belle.

Although every inch of my body is on red flag alert, logic tells me that it's my guilt and paranoia that's making me so nervous. He has nothing, and if anyone is used to having people try to intrude into their psyche, it's me. Dorothy has been assuming she knows all about my twisted inner workings for years.

"Okay then, let's do this your way." I finally find the strength to speak, trying my damnedest to keep playing it cool. "I'll play along with whatever weird logic or opinion you have about me, and I'll even toy with the idea of your proposition . . . on one condition."

"Name it."

He forms that wide, confident grin of his, and again, he leans forward onto his elbows, pressing his chin to his fingers.

"You have to answer every question I have about the woman I watched you propose to the other night."

Mac tilts his head to the side in order to look at me from the corner of his eyes. He's contemplating and assessing the situation. I can practically see the wheels turning in his head.

"I met Lorraine a few years after that writing conference I told you about. I decided to date her because she looked just like you, and I was fascinated by that. I fell in love with her unexpectedly, and now, here we are." He pauses. "Any other questions?"

"Wow," I'm stunned to near speechlessness. "You're not one for small talk are you?"

"Nope."

"Honestly, I don't know whether to be flattered or creeped out. And yes, there are more questions, but now, I'm kind of afraid to ask."

"Are you ready for my proposition, then?" he asks.

"Probably not," I answer.

"Good, because I don't think I'm ready to give it to you, in full, just yet anyway."

"What do you mean?"

Mac picks up his phone from the table to check the time before rubbing at his wrist like he's used to having a watch instead. Then, he pulls a pen from the inside pocket of his jacket and begins jotting an address down onto a napkin as he talks. I watch his hands closely, recalling my image of them squeezing the life from another human. His confidence is unsettling, and the brutally honest confession about his fiancé has left the weight of a rock in my belly.

"I was a failure as a writer, just like you've been a failure at a second attempt in writing. I want to give it another go, but I lack the proper inspiration, just like you. I think we need to take physical action and then write about it, as a team. You and I together. My proposition is more like a plan, and I'd love to talk more about it, if you're willing. Meet me at this address. No phone calls, no more meetups. I'm not going to eat here anymore, now that we've spoken. Don't call me; don't seek out my business. We can't have any ties to one another. No links. No evidence. If you want to talk, just meet me at this address Saturday morning, same time as today."

He hands over the napkin, but not before looking over each shoulder and out the window to make sure no one is watching. I slip it quickly into my pocket. I feel sneaky, filthy even; yet in a weird way, it's thrilling and sexy. A foreign heat pools in my lower belly. Every inch of my body feels the warmth from his fingers as they brush against mine.

"No evidence? What exactly are you talking about?" I whisper.

Mac only flashes me his confident smile before he rises and casually saunters off. He leaves me behind, as if our entire conversation never happened. I'm now sitting on display alone, feeling naked and vulnerable for the whole world to see. I grab up my dirtied plate and take it to the back. My mind is running in circles trying to come up with whatever lie I'm going to feed Lucy. Hopefully, I can pull it off, and fast; Douglas will be here any minute.

Lucy's busy mixing and blending some sort of sugary deliciousness, moving at the pace of a cheetah. We talk just loud enough to be heard over the sounds of running water, clanking dishes, and blending motors, but not so loud as to be heard by customers.

"Is he gone?" she asks with excitement rays shooting at me from her eyes.

"Yeah."

I rinse my own plate and place it in a rack that is soon to be ran through a gigantic dish steamer.

"So? What did he say?" she drills me without taking so much as one breath. "What did you ask him?"

I clear my throat, but she continues before I have a chance to talk.

"That was the weirdest conversation by the door! I knew he had an agenda; I knew it, Ahnia. He *has* been coming here for you, hasn't he?"

Lucy's words pour out of her mouth a hundred miles an hour. I can hardly keep up, let alone interject anything of my own. Her questions assault me, and my stomach flips.

"I think he's kind of a weirdo, Lucy. I told him not to come here anymore."

"What!? Why would you tell him that? Did you ask him about his fiancé?"

"Wow, one question at a time."

"Start with the girl."

"He said he started seeing her because she looks like me, and then he fell in love with her. It weirded me out, so I told him to quit coming here and to leave me alone."

"Oh my God, that is creepy."

"Yeah," I agree, avoiding eye contact.

I can feel her stare at me, eyes narrowed like she does when she's speculating. So far, I've only somewhat lied to her. It feels like the napkin in my pocket is burning a hole straight through my leg. She sets down her kitchen utensils and throws her fists on her hips.

"There's more. You're not telling me everything, are you?"

Lucy never gives up on anything. *What do I say?* My mind is on a reel. Luckily, I'm saved by the gruff ring of Madge's voice as she interrupts.

"Busy morning, Ahnia. Douglas is here for you."

Thank you, Douglas, I think. Even if he does wind up quitting me today, I may just kiss him for saving me from Lucy's inquisitions. I duck my head, dodging any further questions or comments, and rush by Madge, thanking her on my way past.

It looks like Douglas has packed on more than a few pounds. The buttons on his 1980s corduroy suit are working extra hard to stay done up in the middle. His cotton undershirt is peeking through the gaps as if it's trying to escape, and his pants float a couple inches from the top of his dress shoes. A smack of guilt for Douglas' lack of nicer attire slaps me across the face.

If Douglas were to ever kill someone, he'd likely stick around the body for some time afterward. Not to soak up the evil pride of it all, but to cry in self-pity over his actions and to doubt himself as a man. He'd probably find himself dangling at the wrong end of a looped rope over the whole scenario.

"Ahnia." He stands to greet me and slides out a chair. "I'm glad you finally decided to see me."

The pity-melt of his eyes doesn't match his words or offer any encouragement for that matter. He isn't glad; that's a bold-faced lie. I fumble for an excuse.

"Yeah, sorry I've been so hard to get ahold of."

I look at my feet, embarrassed.

"It's fine, it's fine. Let's just get right to business, shall we? I don't want to keep you."

"Yes, please," I agree and take a seat.

It's worse than I thought. Not only does Douglas quit, but he informs me that my literary agent has also given up on my representation. He passes on a direct message from her that if I do ever come up with another book, I'll have to start at square one.

Apparently, she was too busy burying her head in the sand to tell me herself, so she had to pass the news on through Douglas. I'm no longer a shoe-in to traditionally publish a second book. The news hits me like a bullet. A quick, painful jolt to the chest, leaving a hollowed out hole clear through.

I stare off into space, refusing to look at Douglas while it sinks in. I hear the words he says, but I have no response. Then, through the fog of it all, Mac's face is all I can see. Front and center through my mind's eye, he grins at me. I don't even hear Douglas anymore, only Mac. As odd as it was, his proposition swirls around me like a tornado. *We have to take action and write about it, as a team.*

Maybe Mac is right. It was Belle, and what I'd done to her that inspired my best seller. Maybe I do need to take action. My skin crawls, and despite how nasty it feels and how confused I am, it just might work. I'm desperate, I'm lost, and I'm broke. Mac could be my writing career's only hope at redemption. What if he could help me get on top again? I'll do it. I'll keep whatever his little plan is a secret, and I'll meet with him.

CHAPTER FIVE

I don't take this drive any more often than I have to. Dad's house hasn't exactly felt like home since it's lacked the presence of Mom. It especially hasn't felt like home since Dorothy moved in. Tim goes to dinner at Dad's every single week. The typical Friday night as a bachelor without a social life outside of school, I suppose. Waiting on Saturday to roll around, so I can meet up with Mac, has made me anxious, so I decided to take Tim up on the invitation to join them tonight.

What's worse than visiting the house I grew up in is the driving past of one house in particular on the way there. The house *it* happened in. The house I repeatedly sleepwalked to, until one night I did the unthinkable. The house Tim followed me to, but wasn't fast enough to stop the disgusting event that played out.

I ease off of the gas pedal some, just enough to creep past Belle's childhood home at a snail's pace. The windows are boarded up. There are a few deep cracks between the bricks. One of them starts just above a window on the first floor and sprouts like the branches of a dead tree all the way through the second level. Thick weeds and unkempt shrubbery cover the ground, and nearly all of the paint on the front door is faded and cracked, causing it to peel away from the wood as if it's poisoned.

No one has lived there since a mere few days after *it* happened. Belle's father was arrested for her murder and sat in jail until his trial three months later. The police had found inappropriate pictures of Belle hidden away in his underwear drawer. They deemed this enough evidence to prove him guilty in the court of law for Belle's murder. There was no forced entry and no murder weapon to be found. Belle's dad was coming down from a three-day heroin high when a neighbor called the police. When the cops showed up and ultimately found the crime scene, Belle had been dead for days.

In reality, Belle had been abused by her own father and then murdered by a girl she'd been close to as a toddler.

Mom was friends with Belle's mother before she divorced Belle's disgusting father. If only Belle's mom had taken her with, as she did the three older brothers, then none of it would have ever happened. No one really understood the motive behind Belle's abandonment with her dad. It made no sense. Aside from Belle's new stepdad wanting nothing to do with her and everything to do with the boys, there was no reasoning to the fact that Belle's mom left her behind.

Belle became distant from all of her friends. She dressed in only black and refused to look anyone in the eye for years. We stopped being friends, and until Charles paid her so much attention, I tried not to give her much thought. Especially since we were so close in looks. At the time, the whole idea of Belle and her entire family just rubbed me the wrong way.

For the first couple of years after the divorce of her parents, Belle's brothers would visit here and there. That quickly faded; I vaguely remember them, and if they ever did actually come around, they'd recluse. We were really young, and there has been too much that's happened since. I wonder about them all so often now. Dad, Tim, and I went to Belle's funeral. Even though it was less than a week after Mom's service, Dad still insisted we be there. We were close as young children after all.

Belle's family wasn't even there.

I'll never forget the day she was lowered into the ground. I searched for anyone who really loved her, but no such person existed. No mother, no siblings. The casket was surrounded by members of the community who pulled together out of sympathy and shock from the incident. Pretending to be surprised at what "that man had done."

I remember everything everyone said. The comments, the shaking of heads, and especially the lack of love and tears shed for Belle. A not-so-innocent man was locked away for a crime he didn't commit. I walked away free and clear with the loss of my own mother to remind me of my sleepy mistake, every single day, for the rest of my life.

My mom's voice of reason whispers in my ear, *"Ahnia, don't dwell. Always move forward in life. Remember that."* She'd tell me this every time I made a mistake in school, or when I'd break a toy. A hint of sadness was usually hidden in the crows feet surrounding her eyes as she said it. Mom's battle with depression gave her a first-hand view of my struggles-to-be in life. She knew me better than I knew myself, and because of me, she's dead. Because of Belle and the horrid thing I did to her in the very house I'm driving by.

A shiver runs through my entire body as it does every time I pass the house. It starts in my feet and makes its way up and out the top of my head and the tips of my fingers. I turn my focus back to the road and push away the recollection of the moment Tim had to violently wake me. Thoughts of her bashed in head and the blood soaked through my clothes give me a sudden, queasy feeling in my guts.

Tim's Jeep is already at Dad's, parked on the road as to leave an open space in the driveway for me. I chuckle about his unnecessary kindness, as usual. I slip out of my car and saunter to the front door. Dad tries to insist that I come in the garage door like everyone else, but I refuse. That would indicate my being at ease, at home. I'd rather use the front door as any other guest coming for a visit. I ring the doorbell and wait for Dorothy to answer it. She usually does.

Dad hasn't answered the door in years. Dorothy insists on assessing and evaluating visitors before allowing them inside her home. "Too many people simply have too many secrets," she tells him. "I'm a professional. You just stay seated, and I'll be the judge on whether or not they should be allowed as our guests."

What a judgmental hag, I think while waiting patiently in my rightful place on the porch. I listen to the doorbell bounce from room to room in a melodious echoing pattern. It only reminds me of just how big this house really is. What once was an admiration of my father's success is now an insulting slap to the face.

I fiddle with the hem on the bottom of my overworn Nirvana t-shirt. My heel taps the concrete step with my thick knee-high boots as they hug tightly to my ripped skinny jeans. One of the easiest ways to say "F-you" to Dorothy is by showing up to dinner in an outfit that is "less-than-worthy dinner attire.'" Naturally, I go right for the grungiest choices I own.

I used to want this. A big, beautiful, six-bedroom house, fully equipped with expanded living spaces, vaulted ceilings, and a personalized bathroom to fit the needs of practically every guest who might possibly stop in. If not in this exact same suburb, then at least one like it, with only one road leading in and out.

The layout of this neighborhood allows you to admire the gradual size increase of each home as the road snakes up a side hill overlooking the valley. I spent the majority of my childhood imagining my own place here. I even had the color of stucco I wanted all picked out, along with the perfectly grouted rock fence in the back.

Thank God I grew out of that little fantasy. A place outside the city with plenty of garden space, fruit trees, and privacy would suit me just fine. The home itself wouldn't even need to be big. A one-story house with a large, open living space and a beautiful kitchen, the kind of kitchen my mother could have lost herself in. I may not have carried on her culinary skills, but I would never buy a house that didn't honor her memory in the worthiest way I could manage.

Other than that, nothing much matters in a house to me. As I'm allowing myself to get swept away in thought over what has been and may never be, the door swings wide open, revealing Tim's large, crooked grin.

"You came!" he chirps.

"You're sweaty," I reply.

"Dad and I have been playing tennis on the Wii." He chuckles. "Care to join?"

I shuffle in the door, shimmy out of my light jacket and hang it on a stand-alone coat hanger in the corner of the entrance. I look both ways, peering into the sitting room on my left, and then into the first of two family dens on my right. The more formal of the two contains Dorothy.

She's standing as straight as an arrow, donning the hat of a well-groomed homemaker. There are at least a dozen house-plants arranged perfectly on decorative, metal, stacked tiers. They cover the entire wall that's touched by the sun's rays daily from a giant bay window across the way. Dorothy, with a spray bottle in hand, is giving each vine and sprout a squirt. One at a time, she sprays them, and then fluffs the wet leaves like a pillow.

To the right, in the den, is Dad. He's collapsed on the couch, practically laying off of the edge. His arms are relaxed flat to his sides and his legs are motionless, extending straight to the floor. He's huffing and puffing for air with a smile the size of Texas across his face. He must have won a game or two because he'd never be such a happy loser.

I lift a quizzical brow at Tim.

"Do you even need to ask?"

"I suppose not."

We both look back over at Dorothy, who pretends she can't hear a word we say from a few yards away. No hello, or how've you been . . . nothing. She only straightens her back even higher, if that's possible, pulling the crown of her head to the ceiling. Then she gives a few more leaves a squirt. My eyes round a full circle before I give Tim's shoulder a little shove.

"You ready to lose?"

Dad slowly makes his way to his feet, pushing off of the couch cushions with his tired arms shaking at the elbows and grunting along the way. He hands me the other paddle before pulling me into a tight one-armed hug and plants a kiss on my forehead.

"Glad you could make it, beautiful."

I take a long adoring look into his aging eyes.

"Me too, Dad." I smile.

"Now, if you'll excuse me, I have to check the lasagna and step away from this foul game while I have the upper hand and my dignity is still intact."

"You got lucky, old man," Tim says.

Dad giggles and pats Tim on the shoulder before trudging

off, still trying to catch his breath. I lean in close to Tim and whisper toward his ear once Dad is out of ear range.

"You let him win, didn't you?"

"Of course," he replies, even quieter. "He's a stubborn ass and tries too hard. I thought if I didn't back down and stop the game, he'd likely have a heart attack."

We both laugh, and I drop my head to the palm of my hand. Tim lets out an adorable post-laugh snort and then drapes an arm around my shoulders. Dorothy still hasn't attempted to make as much as a sliver of eye contact. I, of course, have no intention of going out of my way to say hello, which is obviously what she's silently digging for. Instead, I spin in a rush and race Tim to the start button on our game, hoping to score a point and one up him before he can get his hands on a paddle.

Not that I need to score any cheat points. I've beat Tim at every single game of tennis we've ever played, be it real or virtual. I loved tennis growing up and was truly a force to be reckoned with on the court. Tim's never stood a chance. Basketball has always been more of Tim's forte. Put a paddle in his hands, and he turns into an awkward, gangly lunatic. It kind of seems like he's swinging at an invisible bug with a fly swatter.

Dad makes it back just in time to witness my winning score and to stick around for one more game, cheering on the underdog. His whoops and at-a-boy comments do no good. I don't even take it easy on Tim; there's really no point. Just as we're packing it in and calling it quits, Dorothy finally graces us with her presence.

She stands behind Dad's leather recliner with squared shoulders and her hands crossed over one another behind him. As Tim and I are moving the coffee table back to its rightful place in the middle of the room, Dorothy clears her throat and announces that dinner is ready.

I look over just in time to watch my dad reach crosswise over himself and place a loving hand on top of hers. He looks up at her with a sparkle in his eye. He's happy, content, and for the first time in a long time, I'm actually grateful for Dorothy. Despite the fact that she's so uppity and judgmental, for some reason, he does love her.

She's kept him from being alone all these years, and I can see in the exchange of her glance that the feeling is mutual. It's my fault Mom's gone, so Dad's happiness is the least I can hope for. Dorothy nods slightly as if to show an understanding of some unspoken gesture before shuffling away.

"Go on ahead, Tim," Dad says. "We'll be right behind you."

I can feel the outside edges of my face bunch in toward the center. If it wasn't for the relaxed lift of Dad's brows and the kind half-smile forming on his lips, I'd have thought this was an ambush. He places his strong but gentle hands on both of my shoulders and smiles. A strange feeling of uplifting comfort washes over me; it's something that I'm not exactly used to.

"Thank you for coming today, Ahnia. I know things have been a little hard for you lately; I've spoken with Douglas."

My shoulders drop a few inches under his hands. The feeling of comfort in them is suddenly gone, and it's replaced with the weight of a semi. I groan and let my head fall back dramatically.

"Please, Dad, can we *not* talk about this right now?"

He removes his hands, and dumps them in his pockets. Before I can maneuver around him and escape toward the heavenly scent coming from down the hall, he says the one thing I've spent the majority of my adult life praying to never hear.

"You know, you're always welcome here, Ahnia. If you ever need money, or a place to stay, please don't hesitate to ask."

I swallow a hard lump and look down at my feet.

"Thanks, Dad," I mutter.

The feeling of failure kneads its way through my bowels. Luckily, he doesn't push it any further. He only gives me another squeeze and then offers me the hook of his elbow. I slide my arm through it and embrace the silence while he leads me to the kitchen.

The lasagna is superb. It's always been my favorite dish, and Dad can cook it better than any others I've tasted. I all but lick my plate clean, like a dog, once I've finished a second helping. I'm stuffed enough that I'm forced to decline a slice of chocolate cake Dorothy picked up for dessert. Baked by Lucy, no doubt.

"So, Ahnia," Dorothy pipes up, "What exactly are your intentions? You know, for the immediate future?"

She flashes me a callous grin before her teeth sink into a forkful of chocolaty goodness. Dad clears his throat and flashes her a warning glare, but he doesn't say a word. Tim's wide eyes float back and forth between the two of us, waiting for some kind of explosion.

"What do you mean?" I growl.

She swallows and then dabs a white, cloth napkin at the corners of her lips.

"Have you considered submitting any applications for jobs, or possibly going back to school?"

"Nope." I smile a toothy grin.

"Hmm, well, perhaps if you took a creative writing class, you'd be inspired."

"Dorothy," Dad interjects, "I'm not really sure we should push any . . ."

"No, Dad, it's fine."

I interrupt him calmly, trying my best to portray myself as confidently as Dorothy does. I even square my shoulders to match her own.

"I've actually started on a project that I'm really excited about. I think I'll be ready to knock out another book soon enough that school won't be necessary."

Tim's head jerks in my direction.

"Really?!" his voice cracks. "Why didn't you say anything? That's great!"

"Well," I ponder on his questions for a moment with Mac's face in my thoughts for reinsurance, "I don't know; I thought it could be a surprise, I guess."

The lie came too easy, and I have zero guilt. I'm relieved that no one presses me even further. Dad reaches his long arm over and gives the back of my shoulder a firm smack. The glee in his face says everything I need to know.

This is my chance. Mac better have something good in mind, because now, I have to follow through. I couldn't bear to let Tim or Dad down now. Besides, I'm really looking forward to giving Dorothy something to choke on.

CHAPTER SIX

I t came as a shock, but getting up early this morning has
been no struggle at all. I even woke up an hour before the
alarm was set to go off. Instead of forcing my eyes back shut, as
I normally would, I pull myself to my feet and start the process
of getting ready for the day.

Makeup is a rarity for me, but today, the mood calls for it. I
want to feel confident and ready to conquer whatever shenani-
gans Mac has in mind. Hopefully it isn't anything too nasty . . .
just nasty enough for the right writing inspiration. I think about
Belle while I line my eyes perfectly with liquid black. I remind
myself that despite her death, it was in fact the action of killing
her that inspired my first book. The book was dark, it was sinis-
ter, and it was a compelling hit. I also remind myself that Mac
is completely unaware of Belle's death at my hand, and whatever inspiring action he's talking about had better be good
enough to count.

I finish up by smoothing the last few wavy strands of my
hair with a flat iron. Pulling it straight brings out the shine and
reveals the impressive length of it. I feel my sexiest with

straightened hair as it flows to my lower back. I shimmy into my favorite skinny jeans and a fitted black halter top before digging through my nightstand for *the* napkin.

The address is on the outskirts of town. There's nothing there but rundown, abandoned housing units and a few condemned factories. This part of town has been ghostly for years. No one goes there aside from a few homeless people, desperate enough to brave the heavily polluted industrial wasteland in order to squat under some broken, leaky roof. It's odd that this is where he chose to meet, but so be it. He did say he wanted our meeting to be a secret. There's no better place in this entire state to remain hidden than a neighborhood avoided by even the majority of the homeless.

I program the address into my phone and then debate on lighting the napkin on fire to cover my trail. Ultimately, I decide against it. I do still have a pinch of speculation. It feels like a little fearful bird is flapping its wings in my belly, trying to escape. I wind up leaving the address out in the open on my kitchen counter between a couple stacks of Ruth Ware and Colleen Hoover novels.

The only people who have a key to my apartment, or that would ever help themselves in anyway, are Tim and Lucy. Neither would show up and do such a thing unless I'd gone missing for a week, or even longer. If that winds up being the case, I may want to leave them the clue.

I lock up and hit the road. It's early, and I'm as ready as I'll ever be. My backpack is fully equipped with a couple of granola bars, along with my computer and murder notes, just in case. I stop only for coffee on the way and fiddle with my fingers on the steering wheel. The road becomes increasingly damaged as I pass several abandoned factories. Broken glass is shattered periodically on the bumpy pavement; potholes and cracks make the drive a rocky one.

A winding road twists past one last parking lot before toxic industry transforms to emptied suburb. The houses are rundown, roofs are caved in, and windows are broken and boarded up. One house after another, the doom and gloom of abandonment has consumed this part of the city like a plague. There is no sign of life. Lawns have turned to dirt and weeds. There are no flowers, no children riding their bicycles on the sidewalks, and no sprinklers dampening the ground. All the things I love about early summer are absent.

There are several houses with the inner walls showing. Doorless frames reveal graffiti and burn stains from being occupied by riff-raff and hoodlums, no doubt. Even they have moved on to a better place. Aside from a few stripped-to-the-frame cars and tumbleweeds, the curbs and driveways are completely empty.

The navigator on my phone leads me through a couple more turns. I don't even bother to stop at the stop signs or yield for crosswalks; there's absolutely no point in that. The blinker is used out of habit only.

Soon, I'm gliding into the driveway of what may have once been a classy home. It's three stories, the tallest on the block, and only half of the windows are boarded up. The others are surprisingly intact, even fairly new looking. The siding is a sun-faded blue, and the shutters are maroon.

Off to the corner of the dirt yard, there's a tire swing. It's hanging by a chain at one side like it was once cared for, yet dragging the hard ground with the other to reveal it's true abandonment.

I imagine a large family once living here. The kids laughing and pushing each other around the tire in a circle while their parents sipped sweet tea in the shade of the opposite side of the tree.

My imagination is a testament of the cruel reality of what

humanity can actually bring about. The smiles would have been slapped from their faces with the foreclosure of their home, their lifestyles, their livelihood. The same happy family of my thoughts could now be standing in a soup line of some random city on the other side of the country. They could be starved, split apart, ripped from the core. And, for what . . . the closing of a factory?

Or worse, the family that once lived here could share a sliver of my own history. Death could have weighed heavily on this family, as it did on my own. Maybe a teen once lived here, a teen that's as twisted as the people I write about in my notebook.

Mac steps out of the front door onto the cracked concrete of the porch. His smile is unfaltering, and it's a punch to my already nervous gut. His clothing is casual yet clean with the tattered fade of his jeans wonderfully intentional. He hooks a thumb at the garage door, nods the same direction with his head, and mouths silent words into the polluted air.

"I'll go open it."

I nod back slowly, awkwardly. *He sure is a strange creature,* I think. Mac, my secret-filled night in tainted armor. There's something about this sneaking around a toxic neighborhood that whispers in my ear to go home, turn around, run away now. At the same time, it's filling me to the brim with the hope of producing a written masterpiece. Along with a strong sense of curiosity in all its beauty and wonder.

I pull my car into the garage as soon as the door lifts. I kill the engine and step out. The large tin door shuts behind me with the push of a button on the wall. Mac, with the same proud grin, is standing in the doorway entrance to our house of mystery.

"You're here," he smiles, "and on time even. I'm impressed."

And, there it is . . . the dig of an insulting compliment.

"Yeah, yeah. Are you going to invite me in before you slice me to pieces? Or are you just going to *off* me now in the garage for easy cleaning?"

He chimes his adorable giggle.

"Come on in. I'm making breakfast."

An unmistakable hum of power generators floats up the basement steps. The stairwell is off to the right, just inside the garage entry. To the left is a small archway past the entrance landing that leads into the kitchen. One ceiling fan with a dim light is powered on in the center of the room. It's hardly enough to light the space as the once sliding glass door to the back wall is boarded shut.

The first thing that comes to mind is carbon monoxide. Shouldn't there be some sort of air ventilation before running a generator inside? Oh well, it is what it is. If I die in this house, at least I left Tim and Lucy the address. Outside, the sun is rising over the hills, creating the most beautiful illumination. Here we are hiding from it behind thick slabs of corkwood over the windows and doors. The kitchen cupboards are made of old cedar and well intact. The pewter countertops are littered with chips, scratches, and burn marks.

I take a seat in one of the two stools that are slid up against a wrap-around countertop, and watch Mac finish crisping the sausage links he has cooking on a portable propane stove. *More gases, lovely.*

"I've got to say, Mac, it's awful here. I don't really like what you've done with the place."

"Aw," he teases back, "but you've yet to see the view."

I set my coffee on the counter, adjust my pack on the floor at my feet, and then pull my laptop out of it. There's clearly no Wi-Fi, so I open a blank word document from the desktop, intending to get right to work. I didn't come here to dilly dally or even to make friends. If anything, I'll keep as far of a distance from Mac as I possibly can. Who knows what he has planned, and complicating things with proximity is utterly out of the question.

I look up as he scoops the sausage onto a couple of paper plates and then pulls a carton of eggs from a small cooler against the wall. He cracks a few into the pan and then pulls out a bundle of grapes. Of course he's bound to be a good cook. If he wasn't a sneak and a phony who happens to be engaged, he'd be the perfect catch. Which reminds me of *her*.

"So, Mac?"

"Yeah?"

"Where's your fiancé? You know . . . that woman who looks like me? What did you call her? Lauren?"

"Lorraine, and she's in New York. She travels for business."

"Your business?"

"Yep, well, our business. She has a pretty face and a lot of attitude, so she's the one we send out to reel in new clients. Tactics."

He turns to face me, while biting down on a juicy grape through an open grin.

"Want one?" he offers.

I only smile and shake my head while wiggling my half-empty coffee in the air. His face drops in irritation.

"Don't tell me you're not going to eat any of this. I've cooked enough breakfast to feed a young polygamist family."

I giggle, unable to help myself. I actually feel strangely at ease; the longer I'm around him the more comfortable I'm becoming. It's like he has some strange, calming power and can hug my soul from the inside.

"Nah," I tell him. "I'll eat. I just usually like to finish my coffee first."

"Good," he says, before pulling a half gallon of orange juice from the cooler and setting it over the top of a giant gouge on the counter. "For after your coffee."

"So what's your big plan, anyway? Did you bribe me to an abandoned wasteland just to feed me breakfast and tell me how pretty your traveling wife-to-be is?"

Mac leans across the counter onto his elbows, closing the distance between us. His gaze is intense, and his facial expression is flat, completely unreadable. A stubbly chin rests on his knuckles. I hold my breath while he stares deep into my eyes. It's quiet enough that I can hear the tick of his fancy Louis Cartier watch. The dark leather fits perfectly slack around his wrist. All I can feel in this very moment is a steady thump of my heart, and I'm acutely aware of the uncomfortable amount of spit in my mouth.

"Nope," he says as he turns back on his heels to flip the eggs. "You're not ready."

"Not ready for what?" I demand, a little irritated that I'm turned on by the intensity of his ego.

"The heist."

I laugh, "The what?"

"Our action, inspiration, writing fall back . . . Our heist."

"You're using me to rob something?"

"Not exactly . . . but kind of."

"I don't get it," I say as I drum my fingers on the damaged counter.

Mac produces an ample plate of deliciousness. I didn't realize just how much I miss breakfast food that isn't either burnt in my attempt to cook or made primarily of sugar. I swallow the last of my coffee and dig in. The flavor is heaven. I shovel down my entire plate as I listen to Mac.

"I haven't decided on the main event just yet. But I think we need danger. We need to do something intense, for real inspiration. We need the feeling of risk in order to write about it. Don't you think?"

Mac's eyes are piercing and lips are pinched. He's hardly touched his food. I think about Belle. He's right; it was the actual feelings of fear, danger, adrenaline, and even confusion that sparked the storyline of my best seller. I had painted my character as being outside of herself, unable to control the impulse to kill . . . just like I had done to Belle in my sleep. It takes some effort to swallow the bite of sausage that's rolling around in my mouth.

"I suppose," I say, before washing it down with a large gulp of juice. "Seems a little reckless, though. I don't know about you, but I don't want to spend the rest of my life in jail because I needed inspiration."

"Which is exactly why we need to research and put together a fail-proof plan."

"Okay, *double 'o' seven*," I exaggerate, "exactly what kind of *research and plan* do you have in mind?"

"Let's finish breakfast." He grins. "Then I'll show you."

As we finish filling our bellies, Mac explains to me how he'd purchased several houses in this part of town through fore-closure auctions when all of the nearby businesses crashed. He bought them for pennies on the dollar under the company name, expecting some sort of pick up or boom in the future. No such turnaround has occurred. Not yet anyway, and practically all the homes are now condemned. Apparently, Mac has dug himself into quite a hole with several business investments, and despite the efforts of his pretty fiancé, MacConell's Marketing is all lined up for the crash of a lifetime.

Mac needs a turnaround just as badly as I do. I can't decide if all this news is frightening or a comfort. On one hand, I know he'll do his best to make something happen, to make our adventure a success. He's not going to back out and stick me with the consequences of our actions because desperate times call for desperate measures. Yet, on the other hand, his judgment is clouded, and I don't know if I should trust his deceiving hands with my entire future.

Mac gives me a short tour up the broken steps of the house, past the second floor, and guides me down a short hallway on the top level. We go into a small bedroom with the stained carpet that's littered from one end to the other with torn pieces of old newspaper. Mac opens the window and climbs out onto the roof. He offers me his hand so that I can follow suit.

The sun is rather blinding. It feels like we're cavemen breaking free from our lives of darkness and solitude. I cover my eyes, place a foot on the windowsill, and let Mac pull me out into the fresh air. My eyes adjust quickly, and I'm stunned at what's before me. Mac wasn't entirely joking when he mentioned the view. I thought he was just kidding around, but wow! It's beautiful up here. I gasp, a little beside myself, and spin a slow circle to see it all.

"Of all the houses I own in Michigan, this, right here, is why I chose this one in particular to work from."

"And by that you mean sneak around?"

"I mean work . . . you and me. Let's get to it, shall we?"

I plop myself down into one of the two beach-style fold-up chairs that are comfortably arranged to face away from the morning sun. Mac helps himself to the other chair. Between us is a coffee table with a well-arranged flower pot on top and two plastic crates shoved underneath.

We're overlooking the entire suburb, plus about half the city, yet we're concealed by the curves and points of the roof. This place is perfect. If I were to live in a house that offered such a rooftop, I'd transform it into a garden deck. The perfect retreat to hide out and escape the world. Mac slides one of the crates closer to him and pulls us each out a pair of binoculars.

"Here," he says, "research time."

"You've got to be shitting me."

"Nope," he says with a voice as cold as stone. "Help yourself. Me casa . . . and all that jazz."

I mumble a "wow" under my breath before reaching for the big eyes.

First thing's first, I locate my apartment building. Just as I suspected, there's a perfect view right into my living room window. I don't say a word, just thank God inside my head that it isn't a view into my bedroom window. I then look for Dad's house, followed by Tim's little off-campus rental. Both are visible, but only in bits and pieces. Surrounding structures block full spying access. Lastly, I focus in on Belle's old home. I hold my breath, ready to lie if Mac asks any questions about where I'm looking and why. Luckily, it's close enough to Dad's place that I could totally get away with it, if need be.

To my surprise, Mac doesn't even seem to care what I'm looking at. He clearly has his own intentions. I place the binoculars on my lap and try to make out where he's pointing his. Of course I could ask, but I'm kind of curious as to what he's willing to tell me on his own. I think it's time for me to sit back and observe for a while, allow myself to process. Mac reaches into the crate again, this time producing a notebook and pen.

"I have a list," he says, "of thieving possibilities."

I sigh; he's really thought this through. I'm not a thief, never have been, and never wanted to be. Even if I did commit a murder in my sleep as a kid, and even if I do daydream about killings as an adult, I still consider myself to be above such nonsense. I kick my feet up to the edge of my seat, and cross one foot over the other. This could be interesting; I might as well make myself comfortable.

"Okay," I tell him, "so let's say I hear you out, and we narrow down your little list. How do we go about the actual act? Wear face masks and kick down doors? I mean, you and I aren't exactly trained in heist tactics, if you catch my drift."

"You might not be, but I've been practicing."

The laughter pours out of me; I can't help it. It isn't just a giggle either. It's a full-on belly laugh, the kind that splits your sides.

"This, I've got to hear," I bellow.

"Over there," Mac points a finger at an old industrial location. There's a large sign stretching across the face of the main building, but the words have been weathered, and even through my binoculars, I can't make out what the name of it was. There are four onsite buildings total. At least one of them must have been a warehouse at some point as it has several loading docks. There's little employee parking, and the entire place is surrounded by an electrical fence topped with spiral barbed wire.

"Yesh! What is that place? Some kind of prison I didn't know existed?"

"It was some sort of government testing lab."

"You sure about that?" I ask.

"Yup. I figured out that it's the only place around here that's still under surveillance of sorts, so I checked it out. You should see the inside. They shut it down over fifteen years ago, but they left behind some pretty crazy shit."

"How the hell could you just figure something like that out?"

"I'm a geek."

"Excuse me?"

"As in a hacker. Didn't you realize that most people in marketing really do know a thing or two about computer systems and how to access restricted databases?"

"Nope, I didn't know that. Lucy has a friend in marketing, and she's an idiot."

"Maybe Lucy's friend is in the wrong business then."

"Maybe you are."

"You're probably right."

I set my binoculars back onto my lap and stare at him. I'm a little surprised, and a little in awe of Mac. He doesn't acknowledge my gawking even one little bit, he only continues to look into his own magnifying spy tool. After a minute of trying to figure him out without success, I, too, turn back to studying the shutdown lab.

"I feel like I don't know you at all," I tell him.

"That's because you don't."

"So what are you? A writer? A marketer? A thief? Or some genius computer hacker in disguise?"

"Ahnia, I'm just a busy man with a high IQ. A guy who over studies, tinkers, over analyzes, and gets little sleep. I think that pretty much sums me up."

"*Humpf.*" I snort an awkward agreement. "So tell me about this place. How do you know what's inside?"

"The surveillance system runs on an old database; the coding was easy to decipher and there are holes. I planted a bug that replays the same fifteen minutes over and over and shut down the power on the north end to cut a hole in the fence. I can only do it periodically and for a few intervals at a time. I've been inside twice now undetected, but I can't do it again for at least a week."

"I'm impressed, Mac . . . a little disturbed, but impressed."

"Why thank you, Ahnia." He grins a full-on, sexy smile in my direction. "Now you know why I'm confident that we can pull off a real job."

"Don't get too full of yourself, just yet. We still don't even have a plan to be so confident about, now do we?"

"I suppose you're right." He scowls out at the wasteland of the suburb below us. "Do you want to see some of the stuff I got out of that place? Maybe we could use some of it, you know, if we come across any emergencies while in action."

He reminds me of an eager kindergarten-aged child ready to show off his pretend spy tools to a friend. For a second, I can't decide if I want to play along or call a babysitter. Curiosity gets the better of me, and I convince myself that a man so muscular and rustic as Mac can act like a child any day of the week; I'd be sure to play along.

"Sure," I giggle.

Mac pulls the other crate from beneath the table. He starts rummaging through it and placing items out on display. There are test tubes and strange chemicals galore.

"Chloroform? Black powder? What the hell are you going to do with all this stuff?" I ask. "I mean, should you even be storing it all together? What if you blow this place up?"

"None of the containers are leaking. I think we're fine."

"Why would you even take this kind of stuff?"

"What do you mean?" His confusion seems genuine.

"It's weird, right?"

"Maybe, but how could I *not* take it?" He scratches his chin. "Could be useful."

I merely shake my head and leave it at that. We move on to talking about danger and creating the feelings we need for writing, something with a real deep-rooted motivation. I'm placing my life in the hands of a genius liar who has access to chloroform. My stomach knots.

How much more danger could I possibly put myself in than this? My mind races to my best seller. No wonder he picked me, I wrote an entire chapter about being numb, a character not in control of her own body. She performed heinous acts, all the while her mind was elsewhere.

I can feel his eyes fixated on me while I recall my own writing. My comparison of what I did to Belle, and what my character did to her victims. I don't know what's going through Mac's head right now, but his grin is growing and calculating. The already stolen contraband, along with Mac's hacking skills and confidence, is filling my head with possibilities. Ideas are flowing like crazy, and writing a fictional book with the incorporation of real life—heart pounding memories, may just work out in my favor, a second time.

I look over Mac's list. There are more than a few shopping centers and a couple of art galleries. To me, none of them actually seem worth the risk. There's a call center that he's likely listed for the equipment. Being a techie, I'm sure he could find a use for the stuff, but anything too big and heavy would be an obvious complication. There's a bank, that's a big fat NO. There's also an old, locally owned jewelry store.

Hmm, now there's something worth hearing him out on. If he's really as smart as he says he is, then we might just be able to pull this off after all. Not to mention the money we could get out of the heist itself. If we were to wait long enough before selling and spending it, as not to get busted, that is.

"I think we should talk more about this jewelry store," I tell him.

CHAPTER SEVEN

I've never really understood why the lighting in furniture stores is always dim and dreary. I mean, I get that they want to create a comfortable ambiance and all, by my hell. If I'm really going to let Dad buy me a new couch today, I'd like to see the exact color I'm about to pick out.

It's been three days since I met up with Mac, and quite honestly it feels like a lifetime. I actually miss him, which is a new feeling for me. We set out to accomplish a bit of homework this week, and intend on following through with our mission this coming Saturday. We'll meet up first thing that morning, study up on the plan A, along with plan B or whatever other emergency scenarios we can come up with, and then execute at nightfall.

I have my doubts. In fact, I'm scared out of my damn mind. But, what other choice do I have? Besides, if we go in prepared and just get the job done quick and easy, then our chances of getting away unscathed are totally possible. I don't know if it's because I'm completely hypnotized by Mac's confidence, or if I truly have unwavering faith in him that I intend on following this through. He's my last hope at a second chance, and I'm not going to pass it up now.

No matter how nervous I am, it's time to take action on something big. We have no intention of selling the stolen goods any time soon. We'd get caught, for sure. We only plan to put it in a safe place, for at least a decade until the coast is clear. I made that my very unmistakable stipulation, in agreeing to such an outrageous 'business' decision. At first, the money has to come from a novel, not the heist contraband. *Just like with Belle, no one can know from where the motivation was rooted.*

The time crunch is an enormous obstacle. We have to get the job done before little Miss Lorraine gets back from New York, and that's not to mention giving ourselves enough time to write a book about it before we're both completely broke. Novels take time, and time we don't have. This really puts a cramp on our heist prep and execution. There's no time to dick around. It's an in and out job. Rip it off like a bandaid, no matter how scary and painful it is. Then we can reap the reward afterward.

On the plus side, I haven't been stalking Mac's business page anymore, and Lucy hasn't said another word to me about him. My dad is insisting on buying me a new couch as an early birthday present. Apparently, he doesn't care that my birthday isn't for another two months. He and Tim came up with the bright idea of an early gift as encouragement on my book to come. Like maybe if I'm extremely comfortable in my apartment, then I'll stay there and write until I'm finished. If they only knew how much time I *don't* plan on spending there.

I've refused to give them any details about my writing project, obviously, only that it'll be another suspense novel. As if I could get any vaguer than that! It's funny how crime mysteries and psychological thrillers can walk so closely, hand in hand, yet be so very different.

Meanwhile, I've already been compiling ideas for an outline. Perhaps Mac was right, a switch up in genre along with real-life motivation might just be the ticket. My own homework for the week is coming up with characters and major plot points for the book. All the while Mac is breaking the walls of the jewelry store's security system and making a step by step plan of attack.

"Oh, I love this!" Lucy says as she plops herself on the right side of me.

Tim joins us, to my left. "Me too."

They've been wandering around, pretending to find me the perfect wraparound, but I've been watching. Tim's avoiding eye contact, and Lucy's just here to brush her hand against his once in a while, hoping that he'll take the bait. Dad left twenty minutes ago. His taste in furnishings is borderline embarrassing.

He claimed that his knees were bothering him, but I could tell by the endless calls he kept taking from Dorothy that he'd finally had enough. He probably just caved into whatever pressing engagement she had planned for him. He left me his credit card and a spending limit before he kissed me on the forehead and mozied out.

"I like it too," I agree. "This charcoal is a perfect shade. I still feel bad though; I hate letting Dad buy me something this big."

"Don't," Tim says, even though he's never needed a handout . . . not even once in his entire life. "Dad has the money. If anything, blame me. It was my idea anyway."

I punch him in the arm, and he pretends to wince. Lucy giggles, completely beside herself. She rarely hangs out with the two of us together, and now I remember why. She's like a high school girl, crushing on the guy who's looking in the opposite direction. I rub my hand across the leather and kick back the extended length recliner under my toes.

"Yep, I think this is it."

Lucy follows suit, kicking up her feet too.

"If you don't pick this one, I'll have to take your dad up on the offer myself," she says. "I could live on this couch."

"Agreed again," Tim says, before pretending to doze off on it.

I chuckle and shake my head.

"So," Lucy says. "If this is the one, what's your plan next? Wanna do lunch?"

"Nah," I say, "I have a lot of ideas running through my head. If I don't get them out now, they'll be lost."

"No one wants that." Tim chimes in before Lucy has a chance to extend the invitation to him alone. "I should probably go study, too. I have a test tomorrow, and I haven't even cracked open that chapter yet," he says even though he doesn't budge from the kicked back position he's found himself in.

"I can't believe you're taking summer classes too," Lucy swoons. "I think you deserve a break. Do something fun before the real hard stuff. Medical school is going to kick your ass."

"Yeah, Tim," I nudge him and point my eyes in her direction. "Something fun." I grin, showing him every single tooth I can expose, and flash him a wink that Lucy can't see.

He blushes from behind what's meant to be an intentional scowl before sticking his tongue out at me like a five year old.

"You two have the fun," he finally smiles back. "I waited too long to do something for my future. I'd rather just stick to my studies, for now."

Rather than getting up, Tim leans back further, nustling himself into the cushions. The look on his face screams a deep pondering of sorts. He's so weird.

"Suit yourself," I say. "I'm going to buy this beautiful couch and then go check out a WiFi cafe."

There's a shopping complex across the street from Mac's choice for our jewelry heist; it's been nagging at the back of my mind for days. He told me about the cafe inside the complex, but I've yet to check it out as not to show up on any security cameras too many times prior to our big job.

"Maybe a change in scenery will help keep me on my toes while I write. Lucy, have you ever been to that place on 34th?"

"Nope," she says.

"If you're still hungry in a couple hours, I think that's where I'm headed. Give me time to knock out a chapter, and then I'm all yours."

"Perfect!" she beams. "I've never been, but there's a shoe store close by that I've been dying to explore."

"It's a plan," I say. "Enjoy your studies, nerd," I punch Tim a second time in the exact same place as before. "Us girls have stories to make up, and shoes to try on."

"I hope you get a bunion." He mumbles back while rubbing his arm. "See ya, Lucy."

Tim jumps to his feet and makes his way out before Lucy has a chance to say anything but a quick, "bye, Tim."

Good move Tim, I think, *thanks for making things less awkward.* Lucy sighs and shakes her head, before shooting herself back to an upright position on my soon-to-be new couch.

"Do you think he's batting for the other team?" Lucy asks.

I cough and choke a little on my spit. That isn't at all what I expected her to say. Maybe how cute he is, or how badly she wishes he'd give her a chance. I think about it, despite myself . . . it would actually make sense.

"Maybe," I finally share my musing aloud. "I don't know, though. I think he would have said something by now. He doesn't have any reason to hide something like that . . . you know? We'd be supportive, and he knows it."

"Has he ever really had a girlfriend?" she pries.

Oh man, I think, I've got to get out here. Or distract her somehow. This is the last conversation I want to have right now.

"Not that I can think of, actually. You know what though, Lucy? I'm sure if he does ever decide to settle down, you'll be the first girl on his list."

"Yeah..." She trails off, staring into a vast nothingness.

"So, lunch then?"

"Yeah."

"Two hours?"

"Sure."

Lucy still looks utterly lost in thought, but I can't play into it. I pull myself to a stand.

"Okay then," I tell her. "I'm going to go rack up my Dad's credit card, and then I'll meet you there."

Lucy closes her eyes and leans back into the couch, adjusting her hands behind her head with her elbows jolted into the air.

"Do your thaaang, girl . . . I'll be there."

I chuckle and leave her to her peace on my soon-to-be permanent apartment fixture. I pay quickly and then make a beeline across town to the WiFi cafe. My mind is working like a hamster in its wheel. It's running overtime and getting nowhere. Finding a place to leave my car is a pain in the ass, but after a few layers into a parking garage down the road, the deed is done.

I keep my line of sight on my toes to avoid a face shot from the multiple cameras above head throughout the complex. I reach the cafe in no time. I pull open the door with a little bit of effort. It's heavily air conditioned with a lock tight door. The crisp air feels amazing as it slaps me in the face on my way in. It's a modern place with low-hanging lights that hover over a long bar-style booth across the wall. Each seat is fully equipt with charging stations and sun-yellow cushioned seats.

First I order myself a latte. The girl at the register can't be older than twenty. She's all decked out in black, and intentionally pursuing her bold-red lips out like a duck. For a moment, I'm tempted to pull out my notebook and jot down her kills, rather than my laptop for the real project at hand. I can see her with a machine gun, plain as day, taking out every breathing human in this place.

Before I take a seat in my intended corner chair at the WiFi bar, I notice Mac across the room. He's sitting at a rounded, two person booth, alone, and typing so fast on his computer it looks like he's trying to murder it. His eyebrows are nearly touching, and he's gnashing his teeth across the top of his bottom lip. Stressed, yet oh so serene, angelic even. I wonder where his mind is, and if he's cracked any codes.

We made the choice not to acknowledge one another in public, so rather than talking to him, I take a seat. I choose a different spot than my original intention, one a little closer to the exit so that he has to pass me on his way out. Even if he can't talk to me, I'm still curious. I can't help but wonder if he'll have any reaction at all to my being here.

I crack open my laptop, search for the hotspot, and get to work on my outline of possible characters and plot points. Having Mac a few tables away only adds to my creativity. I'm chock full of wonder and anticipation, and I only hope my characters can live up to their task. This book will have to be good. I'll have to write something that the creative curve can feed off of our factual events.

Time flies and, before I know it, I can see Mac out the corner of my eye packing up his goods and rising to his feet. My heart pounds against my rib cage, fighting its way out, and my breath catches in my throat. I fixate my glance on the corner of my computer screen allowing my peripheral to stock him like prey. Only the look in his eye is an inferno of rage . . . himself as the predator. There isn't a chance in hell that a man with such a strong sense of determination could possibly be preyed upon.

He stares past me, the death glare shooting rays of distaste over my shoulder. Just as he's about to reach my booth, his face softens, and he drops a note onto my lap in passing. The motion is smooth . . . professional spy smooth, no one would have noticed had their eyes been glued to his hand. I grab the paper and squeeze it with a tight fist. The door behind my back swings shut with a *woosh* in his exit.

I wait a while after he's gone before I open the paper to read the note. I even go as far as pretending I'm pulling it from my pocket, just in case. In the same choppy handwriting as my previous note, it reads:

The eagle's in flight, ready to land in its nest.

Yours always,
Bond, James Jay
AKA 008
Another AKA . . . 7's awesome brother

I sigh, reading the note a few times over, swooning over the banter. Then I tuck it into my pocket just in time. Lucy plops herself next to me, all *thud* and no finesse. I didn't even notice her walk in. Hopefully, she didn't spot Mac leaving. I was way too busy allowing myself to get lost in the thought of Mac to watch for her at the door. That's twice now that Lucy has intruded on my obsessing over Mac, and twice now that she did it by utter surprise.

It was such a small note, yet it tells me everything I need to know. *I'm screwed.* I'm in over my head. This is real. Not only am I about to commit a nearly incomprehensible heist, or felony, or whatever the hell it is, but I'm doing it with a man I'd rather jump on than run from afterward. *How did I get myself into this?* Lucy breaks my mind free of its temporary cage.

"You come up with anything good?"

My lips bunch to one side and I pretend to scratch my chin in thought with my pointer finger only.

"Yep. The eagle is ready for landing."

"What the hell is that supposed to mean?"

I chuckle awkwardly, almost manic. I allow myself to feel the note on my thigh through my pants. A piece of him that's so close to my flesh, blocked only by a thin material, and life's circumstance. A piece that I'm yet again hiding from Lucy, in my jean pocket nonetheless. Oh, the cliche in it all.

"Nothing," I lie. "Just nerdy book stuff. Soooooo, shoes?"

CHAPTER EIGHT

I t's Thursday evening. There are only two more nights
before I meet up with Mac, and I've found myself pacing
the floors of my apartment like a caged animal. The carpet
directly in front of my beautiful new wraparound is wearing
thin already; I hope it survives. I didn't shower this morning
and haven't washed my hair in a few days. I know I'm a sight,
but couldn't care less, really. No one comes here, and I have no
intention of going out. I'm locked in for the long haul.

There was a full week that my mom locked herself in her
room once; I was thirteen. I remember it like yesterday. She'd
had a downward emotional spiral after losing business to a
neighboring bakery. After my dad had delivered her food and
drinks to the room for seven whole days, I decided that enough
was enough.

I sat outside of her room and sang, 'You Are My Sunshine'
for hours until the door creaked open and she emerged. She
dropped to her knees and completely engulfed me in her arms.
Her hair was as greasy as mine is now, and her puffy eyes
matched mine to a 'T.' It was our song, as mother and daughter.

It was the lullaby she sang to me as a baby, and the first song I recited word for word as a toddler.

Like mother, like daughter, I resort to hiding away from the world when times get too hard to handle. Only this time she isn't there for me the way I was there for her. I have no one singing to me from outside the door, no mom to be comforted by. No one to hug so tightly, as I pull myself out of the introverted trance I find myself in. I haven't allowed myself to listen to that song, let alone mutter the lyrics out loud since I sang along to it at her funeral.

Yesterday, I took a fairly large box of donuts from the eatery. Between that and the junk food in my otherwise empty pantry, I have enough food to hold me over. I told Lucy this afternoon that I think I'm catching a bit of a cold. I figure that oughta keep her at a distance, at least until after the weekend is out of the way.

She has a thing about boogers. The last time I got sick, she left a can of soup in front of my door. She rang the bell and ran for it. Aside from an occasional text, I think I'll be safe from her nosey ways. Tim doesn't have classes for a few days, but I'm certain he'll be locking himself away to study, nonetheless, and Dad usually keeps a respectful distance.

With all of my bases covered, I should be able to stress and stew in filth all that I need to before Saturday rolls around and I'm forced to clean up. At that point, I'll face my demise like the brave hero I intend on pretending to be.

A small tap on my door intrudes in on my paranoid thoughts. My chest drops. *Maybe it's a neighbor, weird.* I peek out the peephole, and to my nervous surprise, it's none other than Mac. *He's breaking the rules, idiot! What the hell is he doing at my apartment?*

I rush to a small mirror on my wall, a few feet from the door. After re-pulling my hair even tighter into its messy bun, I scrub my pointer finger across my teeth. Good enough. There's no fixing my look in such little time. I smack my cheeks to make them a little pink. *How embarrassing!*

I rip the door open just as he lifts a hand to knock on it again. With a closed fist around his shirt, I pull him in as quickly as I can.

"You're not supposed to be here," I say before sticking my head out and looking in both directions down the hall.

I lock the door at the handle, and again with the chain, just to be safe. Then I spin on my heels to look at him. His eyes are red and wild, and his lips are pursed. He smooths the wrinkles I caused on his shirt with a flat palm and shakes his head, disgusted.

"I know it's against the rules, but I had to talk to you. I couldn't wait." He says.

"You couldn't call?" I demand.

"I don't have your number and no, even if I did, I wouldn't call. That would be even stupider than stopping by."

"Maybe you're right," I agree, and stomp back to my place of pacing.

"No one saw me. It's getting dark, and no one here knows me anyway."

He follows me to the living area and plops himself onto a corner seat.

"I think you should sit down," he tells me. "You're making me nervous."

I comply without argument, more than curious as to why he's here.

"Well?" I inquire.

I point my forehead at him, and stare up, waiting for an explanation. I'll take anything he'll give me at this point. Be it encouragement, speculation, whatever words he's willing to part with. I'm desperate for any sort of interaction with him, like a phene waiting for my next fix.

"You need to stop stressing."

"How do you know I'm stressing?"

Mac points a finger at my window. The curtains are wide open to reveal nothing but the neighboring apartment building's sun-warped shingles, and an empty street below. Then it hits me, like a wall of cement. He can see me from his lawn chair on the toxic suburb rooftop! *How could I forget about that?* He's probably been watching me this whole time. Of course he has, and for God only knows how long. I deflate some air like a balloon, letting my shoulders drop a few inches. I have no choice but to accept this for what it is.

"Damn it," I mutter. "Well, you're here. Can I get you anything, a drink maybe?"

"You got whiskey?"

"Nope. I'm an alcoholic. Whiskey is kind of my vice. If I kept it in my home, things might get out of hand. I kinda' have to stick with the light stuff."

Wow, why did I just say that? I look down at my lap and shake my head a little in shame. Not because of my problem, but because I just told him about my problem. What's wrong with me? What's next, a confession about Belle? I can't recall a time when I was so completely unsure of myself. A naked sense of vulnerability is seeping from my every pore.

Mac only nods, a humble understanding with absolutely no sign of judgment. His eyes meet mine, and there's something there. He has something on his mind, something he's not saying. We're like magnets pointed in the wrong direction. Two negatives and two positives. Clearly made from the same material, to accomplish the same tasks, yet impossible to touch together. I'm at least three feet away from him, yet I can feel the heat of our energy barrier as it forces us apart. He sighs in surrender and then turns his gaze back to my opened window.

"I do have beer, though, or water if you'd rather." I offer, trying to break the silence.

"That'll do."

I practically run for the fridge, desperate to get away from the tension. I want him, and I know he wants me. I can feel it. Unless I'm as insane as I've always suspected I could be. Maybe that's it. Maybe I'm losing my mind. Just as I bend to reach into the bottom shelf of my fridge, my mind flashes elsewhere. It's a memory, one I've never had before. I'm standing over Belle's bed, staring at her, the metal pipe gripped tightly in my right hand.

She's fast asleep, and just as I rear back to take the first swing at her face, a light flips on. It's a hallway light, just outside of her bedroom door. I don't turn to look; I don't even slow down. My steady and very powerfully driven hands grip the pipe like one would a baseball bat and drop it down on her with full force. Her cheekbone crunches with a splat, and her body begins to twitch.

"You get lost?" Mac's voice rings loudly at my side.

I jump, knocking a cold glass bottle of booze over with my arm. I grab it back up with trembling hands. I straighten myself to a stand and hand it over before grabbing two more for myself. Mac takes a step closer to me no sooner than the fridge door shuts completely.

The scent of him is just as fresh as the first day we met; only tonight there is a muskier underlining. The delicious smell of his natural skin, no doubt. My knees weaken, and I take a step back. The center of my back touches the counter causing me to reach back with my free hand and grab ahold of it for balance.

"What are you doing?" I ask desperately under my breath.

"You were taking a while, so I thought I'd check on you."
His voice is wanting and raspy.

"I'm fine."

I duck and spin, maneuvering my body around him. I'm
careful not to brush our flesh together. He props himself
against the exact spot of the counter that I just left by the hip,
his gaze fixated on me. I look away, twist the top off of my first
drink and guzzle the entire thing as if my life depends on it. He,
too, takes a drink, but barely a sip. The serious clench of his jaw
tells me that he means business. My chest tightens.

"Why are you really here?" I ask.

"A few reasons, actually."

"Which are?"

"I'm trying to decide which one I wanna' tell you first."

He takes another sip and continues to stare. I toss my
empty bottle into the trash can, and twist open the top of my
next. It's quiet enough to hear a pin drop. Aside from my own
heavy breath, I hear only haunting silence.

"Start with whatever it is you're so afraid to say." I breathe,
my heart quickening another pace.

Mac takes a few quick steps forward, again closing the gap
between us. The wildness of his eyes and his hair reminds me
of a lion, ready to pounce. Soon I'm backed against the wall,
with our chests pressed together. I stare at his mouth. His lips
are the perfect shade of pink. I want to lick them. I tuck my
own in and bite the insides lowering my head . . . denying him
access. He places his palms against the wall, beside my shoulders, and lowers his forehead to mine.

"You're not who I thought you were," he says, the hops in
his breath mixing with my own.

I close my eyes tightly and breathe him in. The image I
once had of his fists closing in around the neck of an unknown
man as he shook the life from him is all I can think about. *God,*

I wish I could stop enjoying the thought of death. I can feel his heartbeat through my shirt, and my nipples harden. The heat from his body screams danger, and the pool of nerves between my legs wants it.

"Mac," I whisper, our foreheads still together.

I try and lift my arms to push him away, but can't. Like dead weight, they stay motionless at my sides. I shake my head against his. *This is wrong.*

"Ahnia, I know we can't do this. I just . . . I . . ."

Mac slaps an open palm against the wall. It's an angry, powerful blow a mere foot from my face. I jump, feeling the vibration of it against my entire body.

"Fuck!" He shouts and pulls himself away.

He runs a fist through his hair and storms off. After helping himself to another beer from my fridge, he disappears back into the living room, leaving me behind to gather myself. I take a couple of deep breaths and run my shaking hands down the front of my shirt a few times.

I'm scared to death of him right now, but I don't want him to leave either. I can't kick him out, what if he comes at me? Or worse, what if I wind up throwing myself at him. I don't trust me at this point, any more than I don't trust him.

It takes me a minute to shake the buzz out of my veins enough to actually process what he said. I couldn't possibly be any more confused. I slowly and nervously inch my way back to him. He's standing by the open window, peering down at the street below. On the corner of my couch, the furthest spot away from him, I lower myself to sit. My back is straight and only the back pockets of my jeans touch the furniture's fabric. I'm ready to make a run for it, if needs be. Or, at least, I think I might be.

"What did you mean?" I ask. "When you said I'm not who you thought I was?"

He sighs, "I always thought you'd be more detached than you are."

"Detached?"

"Yeah, like careless. I didn't think you were they type to get nervous or to have a conscience. But, you do."

My voice softens, like a frightened child. "Why would you think that?" I ask.

Mac turns from the window and storms to my side. He's every bit as intense as before. I'm so afraid to look away from his eyes, that I refuse to do so much as blink. I hold my breath. He grabs my hand and squeezes it, tight enough that I know he's serious, but not so tight that it hurts.

"Ahnia, listen to me, and listen carefully."

I nod.

"I told you that I've been your fan since we were teens. I told you that I started seeing Lorraine because she looks just like you. I even told you that I moved here for you. Because *you* are the one I want to work with, remember?"

Again, I nod. This time a little slower, more reserved. A tear pricks at the corner of my eye, but it isn't quite big enough to spill over. I can't tell if I'm frightened or if I'm feeding off of him. I want more.

"You can't back out," he continues. "I've been watching you. I know you're having second thoughts."

"I'm not!" I try to jump in, but he cuts me off.

"You are!" he yells. Then he closes his eyes and purposefully lowers his voice back to its regular tone. "I think we should do this tomorrow."

"What?" I demand as I shake my hand from his. "We're not ready, Mac. You know we're not!"

He meets my eyes again, with the same wildfire burning between us.

"Things have changed," he confesses. "I was able to break

the security wall, so we're as ready as we'll ever be. And . . ." he trails off.

"And, what?"

"Lorraine will be home early. She bombed on our deal, didn't get us the partnership she went for. This could be our only time frame, Ahnia. It's now or never."

"Bitch," I mumble.

I expect a little backlash from my comment, but to my surprise, he isn't fazed by it at all. Not even a wince or sigh. Nothing.

"Besides that, if we wait, you'll back out. I know you will."

The sudden energy in my legs won't allow me to sit any longer. I stand and return to my involuntary back and forth stomping. If what he says is true, then he's right, this could be it. I thought I'd be ready, but I'm not. What if we get caught? What if little Miss Mac-to-be gets home tonight or in the morning, and busts us in the act? Rob a jewelry store, really? What the hell was I thinking agreeing to this? Am I willing to risk my freedom for this? For him?

Mac sits back and watches me. He doesn't fight or try to convince me any further. He merely waits, while I stress and stew. I feel like I'm going to throw up. Then I think of Dad, Douglas, and even Tim, too. I can't disappoint them now that I've told them I have a project. My new memory of Belle and the way I lowered the pipe to her skull gives me a chill. I never would have written my first book had it not been for her. Will I never write a second if I don't commit a new crime?

Mac stands and places his hands on my shoulders, stopping me in my tracks. They're hot and heavy, weighing me down. He's at least a foot taller than me, with an iron board front. I watch his chest as it rises and falls, and will myself not to press my own against his.

"I need to know, Ahnia. I'm not leaving here until you tell me that you're in."

I suck in a breath and whisper, "Okay."

"Meet me at the house at 9."

It isn't a question; it's a command. One that I'll surely oblige. Mac breaks way for the door, leaving the weight of his hands to linger behind on my flesh. He turns back as he grabs the handle.

"Ahnia," I look up, locking eyes. "Take a shower and get some rest. It'll help."

The air catches in my throat. I don't say a word; I just stand there and watch him leave. It feels like the entire world is a tornado and I'm caught right in the middle. That lonesome place in the eye of the storm where it's eerily calm and so loud that it's rendered silent. I'm safe and watching the destruction of my wake take out everything and everyone in my path.

CHAPTER NINE

Mac was right. I did need to shower, and sliding into my clean sheets afterward felt even better. So much so, that I slept like a rock. No tossing and turning. No dreams. No waking in the middle of the night, restless. I must have done enough stressing in the forty minutes Mac was in my apartment that it wore me clean out. The very second my head hit the pillow I was catching every single 'Z' that I so desperately needed.

Right now though, in this very moment, it's a whole different story. The stress is back full force, even stronger. So much for the calm in the eye of the storm. I'm parked a few blocks away from *the* house, practically hyperventilating. I'm late, which I'm sure will set him off, but I can't bring myself to drive these last couple of blocks. My foot is stuck on the floorboard, right in front of the gas pedal.

I don't understand why I'm so nervous. I've been trying to convince myself that it *is* only a robbery after all. Not life and death. *Not like Belle.* I was so confident a few days ago, but not anymore. I wonder if it's Mac that's making me so anxious and not the heist at all.

He's so intense, and the tension between us is overwhelming, suffocating even. I keep thinking of the fire behind his eyes. He has a very dark side, I can feel it. He just keeps it hidden, locked away in some closet somewhere, that no one else has access to.

I imagine what kind of killers people would be all the time, but with him it's different. When I think of Mac as a murderer, it doesn't feel like my imagination at all. It feels more like a hidden memory of sorts or an intuition. There's more to Mac than Mac . . . as if that's possible. More sides of him are unraveling every time I allow myself to be around him, yet I'm hooked. I can't pull away, and I can't seem to run from it. The two of us are a bad mixture. I know that with everything that I am. I know it in my heart and in my head. I can even feel it in my bones.

Suddenly, I realize that this very fear *IS* the reason I'm here. It's the reason I keep coming back. I do, in fact, need the intensity of Mac, and the desire that I have so deeply for him in order to make this book work. He talked about me needing the inspiration of an act in particular, but he was wrong. I need him. I need to feel every part of him before I can put into words the emotion needed to pull off a great novel. A better one than my first.

A grin forms on my face and, for the first time, I'm actually excited about this whole thing. All speculation flies out my window, and I slide the gear stick back into drive. Finally, I'm ready. I'll take whatever he can dish out. After years of watching people, and taking useless notes about my weird imaginings of them, I finally found what I've been looking for. Mac thinks he's using me for a heist, but he couldn't be more wrong. I'm going to use *him*. Whatever he has to offer today, and beyond, it's exactly what I need. This book isn't going to be about a heist at all; it's going to be one hundred percent about Mac and his complexities.

I'll follow through on whatever petty scheme he has in mind for this jewelry store. But, I'm only doing it for what comes after. Mac is in for a surprise because this book isn't going to be at all what he thinks. I'll write what I need to in order to make it work. To make it a hit, just as powerful as my first book. My agent can eat shit and so can Dorothy.

Mac is waiting on the porch when I pull in. He's sitting with his elbows rested at his knees and his face is down with his hands in his hair. I squint to look closer. He's rocking back and forth a little, hardly a motion at all, but it's there. With the sound of my tires in the driveway, he bounces to his feet. My eyes are avoided completely by his. He only runs into the house, slamming the door behind him.

I wait, casually trying to convince myself that I have the upper hand in this whole situation. The garage door slowly lifts, allowing my access. Mac stops it from opening completely, only enough for my car to fit through the crack of it. My antenna nips the metal as I drive in and park. The door is shut behind me before I even have a chance to step out.

"Impatient much?" I ask, as I slam the door and take a step toward him.

I'm expecting him to come back with some sort of snarky remark. I would have preferred that to what I get. He's glaring at my face through angry, bloodshot eyes, but it doesn't feel like he's looking at me at all. It feels more like he's staring past me, at something I can't even see, but that he hates completely.

So much for a healthy dose of Airington sarcasm to start our stressful day. My steps falter, and I hesitate with my hand on the handle of the car door. Perhaps it's intuition or the angry detachment that's radiating off of his body like a force field;

either way, I'm very seriously debating turning around to make a run for it. Had he left the garage door open, the odds of my leaving would be even greater.

I fiddle with my keys while I ask, "Um, Mac, are you okay? You look like you've seen a ghost."

With a closed mouth, he clears his throat.

"Yeah, I'm fine."

The pinch of his lips tells me otherwise. I draw in a deep breath and let it out slowly. *You've got this, Ahnia; you're here to use him, remember?* I try as hard as I can to mentally coach myself and to will my feet to move toward the door, toward him. Finally, he looks up a fraction of a millimeter and lets his eyes meet mine. His shoulders visibly lower, relaxing just a tad, while his chest deflates.

After running a fist through his sexy hair, from his forehead to the crown, he says, "Sorry, I just didn't get much sleep last night."

"Okkkkaaaay," I hesitate some more.

"Come in, please."

I do what he says and follow him inside. The *clip* of my shoes echoes in the silence between us as I take the three concrete steps up. Mac has disappeared inside, invisible from around the backside of the opened door. The sound of the generators down the steps into the basement seem much louder than the other day. There's no mistaking that Mac is now pumping more power into the house than he was before. There's also a scent. I can't place it right off, but the familiarity and rusty underlining of it causes my stomach to flip.

Blood, the realization of the smell clicks into place in my head. It's strong, permeating the air as if it's been lingering for some time. It's like raw meat, that's been sitting on the counter for too long.

"Mac," I whisper, too afraid to say much else.

The door slams shut behind me, and Mac twists the lock. His body is a barricade between me and the exit. Instinctively, I take a sprinting step toward the kitchen, as the basement steps are directly at the opposite side. Before my shoe can make contact with the floor, Mac grabs me up.

With his left arm, Mac has me secured with my back against his body. I kick my feet wildly, they're unable to reach the floor, and the wall is at least a foot away. I can't make contact with anything solid; it's like I'm chasing my own shadow in the air.

Mac has my arms locked to my sides, squeezing me tightly so that I'm completely unable to thrash around. I scream at the top of my lungs, but it's instantly muffled. A wet rag is shoved into my face with Mac's free hand. It's thick and gagging. With eyes wide, I frantically look around, searching for hope or help or really anything that can be useful.

The bottle of Chloroform that he had shown me less than a week ago sits on the counter. My legs slow in motion, becoming numb, one inch at a time. Despite my piqued adrenaline, I can feel the fight in my body losing its umph. I tremble as consciousness begins the escape me.

"Shhhh, my sweet Ahnia," Mac whispers softly in my ear. "Rest now. We have much to talk about when you wake."

CHAPTER TEN

The light is dim. My eyes slowly crack open, and the tingling sensation in my toes and fingers is unnerving. I gasp. It feels like I can't get quite enough air to satisfy the craving of oxygen. It's completely taken over my chest and belly. I'm stuck in a concrete room, and I search it anxiously with my eyeballs only.

My neck won't turn from side to side, and the weight of my head pulls it backward in rest on the back of my chair. My arms and legs are stiff, and my mind is foggy. I'm not quite sure how I got here.

It feels like I'm caught in a dream, a nightmare or even a sleepwalk. My mental facilities are ticking, but I'm lost and detached somehow.

All I can see is the concrete wall in front of me, though I can hear a whimper off to my right side. I think it's a human, but it could easily be an animal. Like a dog whining or even a baby cat. I take a big whiff of the damp air, hoping that a smell of sorts might help me pinpoint what could be making the noise. A rusty, metallic scent creeps its way through my nostrils,

sparking the memory of my arrival to Mac's run-down investment house.

My heart stops, and after skipping a beat, it pounds hard
enough that I can hear it from the inside of my ears. Blood
rushes through my body at an abnormal pace, and I grow light
headed. I think about Mac grabbing me up and shoving that
damp cloth against my nose and mouth. I recall the bottle of
Chloroform he'd left sitting on the counter. Bile rises in my
throat.

Why did he do that? And worse, where am I now?

I close my eyes tightly and focus on drawing slow and
conscious breaths. With one lungful of air after another, I tell
my nerves to calm and focus on the movement of my body.
Whatever this crazy-as-hell man is doing with me, it isn't good.
I was right to be afraid of him, and leery of meeting up today. I
should have told Lucy or Tim about our meeting in the first
place. I could really use Tim's logic and level head right now.

Ting . . . Ting . . . Ting . . .

A slow tapping noise sounds from behind me. I try to shout,
but nothing comes from my mouth except for raspy air. I wiggle
a couple of the fingers on my left hand. I try my best to lift it to
my face, but all that happens is a twitch of my wrist.

"Well, well, well," Mac's voice is low and ominous. "Look
who finally decided to join us."

Us?

I strain my eyes to make clear the image of Mac, as he
comes into my line of vision from behind me. *Chasshhhh*, the
sound of metal dragging across the concrete floor, follows along-
side him. Again, I try to lift my head so that I can find the
culprit of the noise. I focus on my neck, and with all my might I
lift. Rather than the paralleled posture I was aiming for, my
head lolls forward chin to chest. Though I can't lift my head
back up, I can look up from beneath my forehead.

A bat. Mac is dragging a metal baseball bat. I'm also able to see from one side to the other a bit further than before. Barely in my peripheral, I can see the bottom portion of a woman's legs. They're shackled at the ankles to a metal hoop that's bolted to the floor. I try to check my own feet, but am unable to see past my thighs.

She's wearing a black pencil skirt and stilettos. Knees are shaking, and there is a small pool of blood by her feet. I can't turn my head enough to make out the rest of her or to get a look at her face, but there's no doubt that the whimpering was coming from this very woman.

Mac crouches at the knees before me, lowering his face a mere few inches from mine. His breath is hot, and his eyes are filled with spidery crimson blood veins. They're wide, unblinking, and the pupils are gigantic. He's gripping the bat with both hands at the small end, and the larger side is pressed against the floor with his weight.

"Ahnia," he says, "you'll be getting your motor functions back slowly. I'd suggest you pace yourself. You'll need your strength."

I try to speak, to beg, anything. "Wha . . . wha.." I can't get anything out, my voice only cracks and catches in the base of my throat.

"Oh, this?" He asks and rounds the bat in front of his face until it rests on his shoulder. "It isn't exactly a broken pipe. But it'll do."

My stomach lurches and nausea works its way through my body like a title wave. *Belle.* Mac chuckles, before shoving the tips of his fingers against my forehead until it falls back against the back of the chair. I push against his fingers trying to give him some resistance, any resistance, even if it is only a little pressure with my forehead. I'll fight any way I can.

The woman to my side moans a little louder than her

99

previous whimpers. With a little more success than before, I try my damnedest to look over at her. My neck moves an inch at most, but it's enough. I gasp and blink through the distorted fuzz.

It's Lorraine. She's bound with her arms around her waist, tape over her mouth, and soaked in drying blood from the nose down.

"What," Mac says, "you're surprised?"

I wiggle my toes and move my ankles in tiny circles, followed by a twitch at the knee. The movement confirms my earlier question. I'm most certainly shackled to the floor. Just like Lorraine. Mac loops the bat in circles through the air before pointing it at each of us as he talks.

"Lorraine, meet Ahnia. Ahnia, meet Lorraine."

The nerves in my face must be working in full swing because I can feel the dampness of my tears.

"No!" he yells.

Mac storms toward me like an angry bear and points the bat an inch from my face.

"You're not allowed to do that! *You* can't cry!"

Mac stares at the concrete floor for a moment, his chest rising and falling with angry breaths. Then he begins walking back and forth from one wall to the next, muttering and mumbling something that I can't quite make out. I look back at Lorraine, this time turning my head completely. The blurriness of my vision is clearing, and I'm able to get a better look at her.

She's staring back at me. The fresh tears are washing clear lines through the dried blood on her face. There are black circles around her eyes from the makeup that's been rubbed and cried away. Her body is shaking, and she tries to make words from beneath the tape over her mouth. Mac storms to her. With one swift rip, he frees her lips from their bondage.

After gasping for a full breath, she sobs, "why?"

"Why?" Mac shouts and again points his weapon in my direction. "Why don't you ask her!? Or better yet, let's call my therapist shall we?"

I wiggle at the core and slowly lift my head completely on my own. Finally, I'm able to see all the way around me. There's a tiny video camera sitting on a tripod to my left. Mac continues to shout at his fiancé.

"I told you to stay home! Stay away from this place, and you just wouldn't listen!"

"Mac," I'm finally able to whisper. "What did you do?"

His head rolls back in laughter. The sound of it bellows from him like a crazed maniac. It's loud and rolls from the pit of his stomach.

"What did *I* do?" he asks and laughs again. "What did *I* do!" he draws out and emphasizes the "*I*" each time.

"Mac," Lorraine's voice is intentionally calm and low. "Calling your therapist isn't a bad idea. Look, if this is about your stepdad then we ca . . ."

"Stop," he cuts her off before she can finish. "Stop right there!"

Mac bends at the waste, closing the gap between their faces. "Not another damn word. You understand?"

Lorraine nods her head wildly with her mouth shut, more tears streaming down her face.

"Please don't hurt her," I beg.

Mac turns his head to look at me in one swift motion. The rest of his body still bent toward her. His breath quickens, and I can tell in an instant that he's ready to unleash whatever pent up wrath he's kept inside. He pulls himself to stand tall, tilts his head to one side, and places his free hand in his pocket.

His voice is lowered, calm even.

"She's right you know," he tells me. "My stepdad was a real piece of work."

"What are you talking about?" I sob.

"My mother could really pick 'em."

My heart sinks to the bottom of my stomach. So many things flash through my head it's hard to straighten them out or to focus on one thought at a time. The image of Mac shaking the life from an unknown man comes back again, yet it's real. It seems more prominent, more like a memory than a vision.

I close my eyes tightly and shake my head back and forth. I see it again, yet the man isn't unknown at all; it's Tim. We're young, teens, and we're there in *that* house. The three of us in Belle's room. She's already dead. The bed is soaked in her blood.

The thought is then replaced by another. My body shakes, and my teeth clench. I grind them back and forth, trying to stop the repressed memories as they flood back. I don't know if I was sleepwalking at the time or if I went into the kind of shock that blocks out the events for all these years. *Am I really that psychotic? Am I as twisted as the character in my first book?* I don't know what to think or what to believe anymore.

The entire event flashes across my mind, one clip at a time like a projector, reminding me of what really happened *that* night. I don't remember walking there or sneaking in the window. That part of the night is still lost in the foggy, mix-up of my mind. The reel starts with the flip of a light behind me, just like I remembered while Mac was in my apartment last night.

I knew the light was turned on and I didn't care. I feel it now as if I'm actually there. My body is thawing from the chloroform, and it feels just the same. As if I'm beside myself, excited, cheering me on. I watch in memory as I lower the pipe on Belle's skull. Over and over I bash the life from her. Tim climbs in the window. He's too late, but he makes a run for me anyway. After ripping the pipe from my hands, he shakes my shoulders and yells in my face. I stare back at him blankly with a satisfied smirk.

"Ahnia!" *Clap.* "You in there?" Mac shouts.

I open my eyes, again blurred with tears.

"For a second, I thought I'd lost you."

He teases me with a voice every bit as dark as before.

"You know," he says while grabbing up the camera by the base of its tripod in order to place it closer to me. "The fact that we've actually kept our secret this long is impressive."

I grit my teeth and lie through a tight lip, "I don't know what you're talking about."

"Oh, yes you do," he says. "My stepdad finally died. Liver failure of all things. Go figure. I've been planning this for years, and now that he isn't here to threaten me with my mom's life, I *finally* get to follow through."

"You have to stop this," I beg.

"No, Ahnia! *You* have to stop this!" He shouts again, his voice echoing through the room. "It's time to confess, and you know exactly what I'm talking about!"

"I don't! I swear to God, I don't!"

"That monster compared me to you all these years. I hope you know that. He'd say, *'You're a worthless little bitch, Mackenzie. You'll never have as big 'a balls as that girl who killed your sister.'*"

Mac disappears behind me, and I hold my breath. He comes back with a fold-up chair. A foot in front of me and right next to the camera, he slams the chair down and plops himself into it. Lorraine continues to sob at our side but doesn't say a word. He's straddling the chair backward with his elbows pressed against the top of its backrest, the bat dangling from his hands. I look over at Lorraine, begging with my eyes for help. She looks away, turning her head in the opposite direction.

"What did you do to her?" I whisper.

"Oh, God! So now it's *me* with the problem?"

"She's bleeding."

"She fell up the damn stairs. I had to tie her up so she wouldn't turn me in. The cops can't come! Not yet!"

"What do you mean, yet?"

"Don't tell me you actually thought we were going to rob something?"

I squeeze my eyes shut, trying to avoid his burning gaze. The darkness of my lids provides no comfort, for as soon as they're shut the memory reel continues. It's real, and I'm watching from the outside in, through my head.

As Tim tries unsuccessfully to shake me awake, a very tall man with extremely wide shoulders, a five-o-clock shadow, and an evil grin stumbles into Belle's room. He's the one who flipped on the light. With a half-empty bottle of whiskey in one hand and the collar of teenage Mac's shirt in the other, he struggles to toss Mac toward us.

In a scratchy voice he slurs, "See boy, I told you you'd wanna get outta bed for this."

I hadn't seen Mac or either of his brothers since we were small enough to compare our boogers, learning to tie our own shoes. This teenage Mac looks back and forth between me, Tim, and his dead sister. She's still twitching on her bed. He goes right for Tim, grabbing him by the throat and starts shaking him wildly. I stand there and watch. Not moving, not helping my own brother in the slightest. The twisted grin on my sleepy face is still fully intact.

The tall man chuckles. "That's enough, boy."

He grabs Mac again by the collar and rips him away from Tim. Tim falls to the floor gasping and pawing at his throat. After he catches his breath, he pulls himself back to his feet. Tim doesn't even look at the tall man or at Mac as he kicks and swings trying to escape the man's grasp.

"Wake her up," the man commands, "and get the fuck out of here before their real dad wakes up. I'll keep this little rat quiet. But if either of you talk . . . your whole family will pay for what she did."

I gasp and snap my eyes back open wide. The aged Mac is staring at me, waiting . . . *But, for what?*

"Just say it, Ahnia. Tell the camera what you did."

Sobs roll through me, rocking my shoulders uncontrollably.

"Don't make me use this, Ahnia." He waves the bat in the air.

"I don't know what you're talking about," I whisper the cold-blooded lie through clenched teeth.

"That's enough!"

Mac again stands and disappears behind me. This time, whatever he's pulling across the floor is bigger. The metal dragging over concrete is loud and slow moving. Mac grunts, struggling with the heavy load. I thrash my arms in their restraints the second they come into view. I scream and beg, but it does no good. Mac doesn't even look my way, as he pulls Tim across the floor.

"It's only fair, Ahnia."

He positions the unresponsive Tim on the opposite side of the room. They're hiding behind the camera's view. It's pointed at me, and only me with one purpose. Mac wants a confession, and he'll clearly go to any length to get it.

"You can stop this, you know. All you have to do is say it."

"No!" I beg. "Please don't hurt him! Tim, wake up! Please, wake up!"

Mac laughs.

"Really?" he chuckles, "That's what you're going with right now is, 'wake up'?"

Mac turns, swinging the top half of his entire body with the bat in his hands. It comes down on Tim's knee. The *crunch* of

Tim's kneecap rings through the air, paralyzing the parts of me that have only started to regain feeling. I don't know who screams louder, myself of Lorraine.

"Say it, Ahnia!" Mac shouts over our shrill screams. "Say her name, or the next one will be his head! You took my sister, and I'll take your brother! All you have to do is confess!"

I shake my head back and forth violently.

"No, please!" I sob.

Mac lifts the bat into the air, ready for his next blow.

"Stop!" I shout. "Belle! Her name was Belle!"

EPILOGUE

B*uzzzz* . . .
The digital clock above the bars on my cell reads three-o-seven. It's been four years, three months, two weeks and five days since my conviction. Murder in the first degree. Because I was a juvenile at the time of the killing and received ongoing mental evaluations, the sentence included those nine magical words 'with the possibility of parole based on good behavior.'

Today's the day. I've packed what few belongings I have in a small cardboard box provided by the guards. The buzzer rings every time someone on our block has a door open. I stand before the bars, ready, excited. I tap my foot impatiently.

"Well, Ahnia," Says the guard outside my door, with a chubby yet strong hand planted firmly on her wide hip. "Congratulations. Follow me, please. Your brother, Dr. Airington, is waiting out front."

I comply and follow her with my head down. Lessons learned tell me not to speak back or acknowledge what she's said to me. We pass several hallways, unlocking doors buzz before opening.

I grip my box tightly, thinking of the photos and journals inside of it. Tim and Dad have kept me updated as often as possible, bringing me copies of every family photo I ever requested. They're mostly of Mom. The box also holds several comp journals. I've been busy behind bars and am clinging to the box now like my life depends on it. *I guess in a way my future does.*

The air outside is crisp, refreshing. The smile on Tim's face confirms that today is real, it's happening, I'm free! The limp in his steps reminds me of exactly why I've been stuck here for so long. As Tim wraps his arms around me tightly in a comforting hug, I'm glad that I asked Dad not to come here today. We're meeting him at the eatery in an hour.

I can't wait to sink my teeth into some real food. Lucy will be there too. I haven't seen her since I was arrested, but have been pleased to hear all the fond things Tim tells me about their relationship when he comes to visit.

Tim walks me out and opens the door to his jeep. I'm in awe that he still drives this old gem. I'm tempted to mention it but am still rendered mute from the shock of this entire day. I climb in and watch him limp around to the driver's side. He heaves himself in with his one good leg, and lifts the other with some effort.

"Well . . ." he says, as soon as the door is shut.

Tim stares at me as if I know what he's hinting around about with a single word.

"Well what?" I croak. "I mean . . . thanks, thanks for coming."

Tears stick the back of my eyes, trying to fight their way out.

"No, no, no." He holds a palm into the air, stopping me

before I get carried away. "We have an entire hour's drive. Just you and me. I want you to take a deep breath and read."

"Are you serious?" I question, taken aback by the request. "Already? I mean, don't you want to chat? Maybe talk about Lucy, I'd love to hear abou—"

"Nope." He stops me again. "We have the rest of our lives for that. This can't wait. I want to hear everything you have time to read before you have the time to back out of the entire book now that you're free."

"But, Tim . . ."

He starts the engine. "Read it!"

I sigh, my surrender very clearly painted on my face. I pull the notebooks from my box and flip open the notebook marked with the **number one** and begin.

"Justice for Belle . . . Chapter one . . ."

ABOUT THE AUTHOR

Didi Oviatt is an intuitive soul. She's a wife and mother first, with one son and one daughter. Her thirst to write was developed at an early age, and she never looked back. After digging down deep and getting in touch with her literary self, she's writing mystery/thrillers like *Search For Maylee, Aggravated Momentum, Sketch, and New Age Lamians.* Along with a six-piece short story collection called the *Time Wasters*. She's also collaborated with Kim Knight in an ongoing interactive short story anthology *The Suspenseful Collection.* When Didi doesn't have her nose buried in a book, she can found enjoying a laid back outdoorsy life. Time spent sleeping under the stars, hiking, fishing, and ATVing the back roads of beautiful mountain trails, sun-bathing in the desert heat, along with watching the relaxing dance of a campfire plays an important part of her day-to-day lifestyle.

Didi Oviatt would also like to invite you to enjoy a sample of her cold case mystery, **_SEARCH FOR MAYLEE_**

SEARCH FOR MAYLEE SAMPLE

Autumn drew in a lungful of California air. Although it was thick, it was somehow refreshing. She looked to her side at the sun glistening off small choppy waves on the oceanfront. It sparkled in bright flashes across the horizon. She was really going to miss this stunning morning view. A thin lilac tank-top dampened with sweat in the center of her back. Her feet were growing heavy, but she pushed herself and quickened her stride. Autumn had been running along the beach every day, sometimes a few times a day, for the past three years. She found that running helped to clear her mind, and tiring her body helped her sleep at night.

Every day during this run the thought of Maylee's disappearance raced through Autumn's mind on a loop. Every intricate detail was recalled, in order, exactly as it happened. She remembered what Maylee had eaten for breakfast, and dropping her off at school that morning. Even the conversation they had haunts her.

"Don't you want some eggs?" Maylee chirped in her perky morning voice.

"Nah, I'll just grab a coffee."

"Whatever Aunt Autumn, you're going to sneak one of those disgusting greasy processed breakfast muffins after you drop me off, aren't you?"

Accusing eyes pierced Autumn's embarrassed face, forcing her to blush. Strange, how such a young woman could find so much fault over an innocent guilty pleasure no bigger than a thin slice of cheese with sausage.

These memories continuously float in and out of Autumn's mind, circling her like a consuming shadow, just waiting for the right moment to swallow her whole. After reliving the worst day of her life, Autumn would clear her mind, steady her breath, and convince herself to focus on the present. It felt like an impossible task to stop living in the past. Maylee was Autumn's niece, and she was seventeen years old when she was taken. Maylee was a high school senior with two weeks left until her graduation. She had her entire life ahead of her.

Now, three years later, Autumn was convinced that if she could just remember any tiny detail, something she may have skipped over, the police would be forced to pry Maylee's case back open. Autumn was more of a mother to Maylee than her junkie sister could ever dream of being—even on a sober day.

It had been nearly an hour since today's run commenced. Time seemed to escape Autumn as the worn out sneakers laced to her feet moved further down the beach. Her legs were starting to tingle and burn. They weakened and felt like noodles under her wearying body. The intake of air burned her chest, leaving her throat to feel like a charred tree—still intact and alive, but the edges burnt to a crisp. She could feel the color of her face darken as freshly oxygenated blood sped through her veins.

Over the course of the last few days, she had pushed herself even further than her usual run. She would be leaving her beautiful home in Northern California and moving to a small cramped one bedroom apartment right in the center of Denver Colorado. Every detail of her life would change once again, and it was terrifying.

Autumn fell into a deep depression when Maylee went missing, and she became obsessed with the case. The only time she would leave the house was to go to the grocery store or police station. Her life's purpose became nothing more than to pester Detective Chance, or just Chance, as everyone called him. His full name and title was Detective Chance Rupert Lizhalia III. Clearly, the comfort of being referred to so casually by his first name was developed very early on in his career. The details and progress of Maylee's case were poked and prodded at by Autumn daily. It was a repetitive process until about five months after Maylee had disappeared. At that point, Chance put Maylee's folder on an overstuffed shelf to collect dust.

"We have done everything we can," he told Autumn on that bizarrely hot fall afternoon as he slowly wiped the sweat from his full, perfectly squared hairline.

"So you're going to throw her away? Just like that, you're done?" Autumn demanded, tears welling.

"Every police station in the country has Maylee's picture." Chance reminded her. "If anyone finds her or comes across anything that we can link to the case, then I assure you, Autumn, you'll be the first to know."

The short conversation had rendered Autumn mute. She stood frozen in shock as he told her to move on with her life. Chance apologized for the loss in such a way that it was clear— Maylee would never be found. Then he brushed past her in the hallway of an over-lit police station and went about his day as if nothing had changed.

Autumn recalled it now as she ran, remembering the cold

emptiness in Chance's expression. The excruciating heat of that day hadn't even touched the icy daggers he sent jabbing into her chest. Even his outfit was seared into her memory. He wore a dark gray suit, complementing his tan, and an orange tie.

There was no denying it; Chance was a very attractive man for his age. The stress of the job was surely the culprit of a cluster of wrinkles at the corners of his eyes, although they only added to his enticing façade. Chance was the kind of man that you could take one look at and just know, without a doubt, he could defend himself. His build was strong enough to be noticed, with broad shoulders and a flat stomach, but his eyes were key. They were light gray and deeply piercing, always with a sharp gaze—like an eagle ready to swoop.

The afternoon Maylee's case was practically declared unsolvable and doomed for a cold shelf life, all hope drained from Autumn. Her car was left in the parking lot, and slow-dragging feet carried her home, she moved in a blurry haze. Amidst the draining three-mile walk to her front porch, the heat transformed into gloom, and before Autumn knew it, she was engulfed in rain. The weather as unforgettably odd.

The door swung open, and she collapsed onto the floor, unable to take in air. Anxiety surged through her body in waves, and salty tears streamed down her face. God only knows how long she lay paralyzed on the floor before she got up and ran out the door. Pushing herself through the stinging oversized drops of rain, she rounded a corner and made her way to the beach. Giant deadly ocean swells had never looked so inviting, but she refused to stop, continuing to run faster. Step after painful step in the sand, she pushed forward.

Oxygen eventually stopped reaching her lungs, and her legs gave out. Several times Autumn collapsed to her knees and stared into the water while she wheezed and struggled for breath. Each time the *slosh* of wet sand sounded beneath her fallen body, she would pick herself back up and continue to run. By the time she returned home, the sky had turned black, and there were no stars to be found. Autumn was completely surrounded by darkness, a perfect match to the way she felt inside.

A haunting recollection of her own swollen, bloodshot eyes staring back at her from the hallway mirror now left an imprint in Autumn's mind. On that traumatizing day, she became a ghost—an empty shell of her once prominent self. Maylee's absence was officially real; there was a sense of finality, a permanence that made Autumn sick.

That night after her first run, the world went completely black. As soon as her head hit the pillow, exhaustion and grief took over, blocking out whatever was left of her subconscious. For the first time in those five miserable months, her body gave up. She had slept an entire night through, deep and dreamless. It was the first night without nightmares and cold sweats since Maylee went missing.

Since that painful day, Autumn continued to repeat that same beachside run. Slowly over time, she's made an effort to put her life back together. So far that effort has proven unsuccessful.

This would be the day Autumn was going to take what could possibly be the biggest step of her life. Giving up on Maylee was not an option. This move was bound to uncover something. It had to. The winding road came upon a corner and revealed a small deserted parking lot. She was close to home now, with only a few more blocks to go before the first 'For Sale' sign came into view. The signs were pointing in the direction of her striking oceanside condo.

Autumn slowed her stride to a heavy-footed jog until she reached the lawn in front of her newly sold home. No sooner than her sneakers sunk into the freshly cut grass, she bent at the core and clutched her knees tightly, knuckles whitening, to catch her breath. Autumn glanced up to notice the front door had been opened a crack. She squinted over the top of her right shoulder, then abruptly to the left, peering down the road as far as she could see. There were no cars out of the ordinary aside from the large U-Haul sitting a few yards away.

Paranoia was common for Autumn. A constant nagging fear weighed in her chest at all times; she was forever burdened by this. It had taken a full year to convince herself to sell all of her belongings and take this giant leap. She had to be strong, and she had to leave California, for Maylee. With caution in each step, Autumn slowly made her way up to the condo. She peeked into each window, then tilted an ever listening ear toward the crack in the door.

"Oh, for hell's sake Autumn, you're such a weirdo! You're going to pack up all of your shit and take off on some 'save the world trek,' and you can't even walk into your own house without panicking!"

The voice was shrill and mocking. It belonged to Candace, Maylee's mother. Autumn exhaled and walked inside. The sight of her sister leaning against the bar that connected the kitchen to the dining room was a lot to take in. Candace was tall and skinny. Too skinny, Autumn noted. One bony leg was crossed over the other, and a thick string of smoke lifted into the air from the cigarette burning between her fingertips. She rolled her eyes at Autumn dramatically and then flicked a long ash onto the floor.

"Candace, do you really need to do that? You know I don't let anyone smoke in my house. You think it's okay to just ash all over the place?"

"Who cares? You sold it anyway."

Candace walked over and ran what was left of her smoldering cigarette under water and dropped it into an otherwise spotless ceramic sink. The condo was empty, making it seem even bigger than usual. Autumn looked around her home, holding back the tears that were soon to inevitably flow—it was only a matter of time. The floors transformed from a dark marbled tile to white carpet in the living room. The ceilings were vaulted, and the countertops were black with marbled gray granite.

Autumn had married at a young age and lost her husband in a car accident shortly after. She had only known Keith for seventeen months total. A vow was made to herself when he died, she would never love another, and that was final. It'd been eighteen years since the accident, and so far she'd stuck to her promise. Autumn went back to her maiden name, Brown, in an effort to help herself move on from the trauma of his death. Keith had come from money and left Autumn a rich young woman at the time.

Initially, she bought the condo along with a dependable used car. Then she placed what was left of the settlement into a steady monthly income that was meant to last 20 years. Since then, the car had been traded in for a newer model, an end of this cash flow was rapidly approaching, and the condo sold. Autumn was trudging unfamiliar ground as her entire life was growing foreign, and that didn't even include her job.

After the loss of her young love, the years passed and the cost of living grew. Her fixed monthly income was barely enough to pay the bills and keep her fed. Enjoying nights out with her girlfriends, or buying new outfits were rare. A few years after Keith passed, Autumn picked up a job working as a waitress in a small crab shack just down the road from her condo. Surprisingly she absolutely adored it. It didn't bring in much money, but it was enough for the little extras, and it kept her busy.

As Autumn stood across from Candace in her freshly

emptied kitchen, her mind wandered to the saddened look of shock on her boss's face when she'd quit. Autumn walked away from the steady job she loved, just over a week before. Candace cleared the tar blockage from her throat, pulling Autumn back to reality.

"How did you get in here?" Autumn asked. "And did you get me that address? I'm leaving soon. I only have a few more things to pack, so I need it. You promised."

"You always leave that window in the back unlocked," Candace said with another roll of her glassed over eyes. "And yes, I have your damn address."

Candace dug a small wrinkled piece of damp paper from her pocket, along with a chunk of dirty pocket lint and a couple of pennies. The goods were slapped onto the empty counter-top. Candace then shifted restlessly on her feet, her eyes darting from one side of her head to the other. The look of a wild animal had taken over her face as if assessing the possibility of an unexpected dash for the door. Unpredictable and permanently on edge, she finally continued in her scratchy smoker's voice.

"I still don't think you should do this. Craig's not a bad guy; he just gets a bad rep because of his record. Maylee's gone because she never paid attention to anything going on around her. It's probably her own fault she was taken, I'm sure Craig had nothing to do with it."

Aside from the obvious itch to leave, Candace was without emotion, utterly careless about Maylee. She spoke as if Maylee wasn't her daughter at all, but some strange girl she'd met on the street. It made Autumn's stomach wrench hearing her sister talk this way about her own child, her flesh and blood. How could she?

The thought of the opened back window was intentionally brushed aside. Autumn didn't even want to know exactly how her sister was privy to that information. The place would be deserted in a few hours, left for the new owners to deal with. The only thing that mattered now was how clearly strung-out and cold blooded Candace was. A surge of anger flowed through Autumn.

Autumn couldn't stand Candace for the evil woman she'd grown into. The fact that Candace cared more about herself and getting her next fix than she did about her own daughter was sickening. Autumn stormed over to the bar and snatched up the piece of paper. It wouldn't be out of the ordinary if Candace were to change her mind, steal back the address, and make a crazy dash for the door. Frankly, it came as quite a shock to Autumn that her junkie sister had actually followed through on her promise to retrieve it in the first place. Once the address was safely in hand, Autumn finally spoke her mind.

"Maylee hated that man and the rest of your friends. She was scared of him! She ended up here ninety percent of the time because you were a shitty mom, and your shitty friends are all terrible people. Open your eyes, Candace; when are you going to understand that he was the only real lead the cops ever had? Now get the hell out of my house!"

Candace took a step back, shocked at Autumn's outburst. Her head tilted forward allowing her eyes to be shaded by the lowering of her brows. The shifty feet that struggled to hold up her stick-like legs for the first time held still. They had gotten in several fights about Maylee over the years. They brawled more since Maylee's disappearance than ever before. Candace knew she hadn't been the best mom to Maylee, but she would never admit it out loud, and she didn't much care either way. Excuses were constantly shelled out for her behavior as she never even wanted a child in the first place. Candace justified her actions to herself in any way she could.

Autumn wasn't the only one with resentment, as Candace

genuinely returned the disdain. For most of their lives, Candace hated her sister for being the pretty one, the favorite. A prominent loathing of Autumn's perfection had taken up residence in Candace. There was even slight anger toward Maylee for confiding in Autumn as much as she did. Candace would leave Maylee for weeks at a time, and then get upset when she would find her at Autumn's house. Maylee was punished whenever her Aunt Autumn was mentioned.

Once Maylee was about twelve years old, Candace finally gave up and no longer asked or showed any concern. Candace couldn't care less whether Maylee came home or not. Candace knew that Autumn's was the only phone number Maylee knew by heart, and that's where she would usually be. There was no point in the chase. Besides, the less Maylee was around, the more freedom there was for her. There were no whiny voices begging for food, or phone calls from teachers complaining about smelly clothes or random bruises.

Candace now stared back at her angry sister contemplating what insult she would throw next. Whether it be about Keith dying, or about their Mom being in a nursing home, she usually thought of the things that would hurt Autumn the most before she spoke.

"You're not going to find her, Autumn. All you're going to do out there is waste what little money you have left and abandon Mom. You're leaving her here to rot while you chase a ghost."

Candace watched closely and fully satisfied as Autumn winced. The fact that their mother would be left all alone pulled fluid to the surface of her eyes. Hannah Brown, Autumn and Candace's mother had lived with Autumn for quite some time after her stroke. Once she became too heavy for Autumn to lift, Hannah was checked into the nicest nursing home within a twenty-mile range. Autumn would visit her on a regular basis. Candace, on the other hand, hadn't seen their mother in years.

Autumn watched her sister strut to the door, then turn to look back as she twisted the door's handle. "Good luck on your mission, Superwoman." Candace sneered, chuckled lightly, and walked out.

Justice For Belle
ISBN: 978-4-86750-341-6

Published by
Next Chapter
1-60-20 Minami-Otsuka
170-0005 Toshima-Ku, Tokyo
+818035793528

4th June 2021